The Steel Orb

The first volume in
a collection of writings by

C.J.S. Hayward

C.J.S. Hayward Publications, Wheaton

1. Orthodox Eastern Church--fiction. 2. Orthodox Eastern Church--spirituality. 3. Orthodox Eastern Church--theology. 4. Orthodox Eastern Church--humor. 5. Time--speculative philosophy. 6. Animals. 7. Science fiction. 8. Fantasy.

ISBN 978-0-6151-9361-8

The reader is invited to visit CJSHayward.com.

Contents

Your Fast Track to Consecration!

Dear Valued Orthodox;

Have you ever thought about being a bishop? Have you thought how special that office would be?

Have you thought it was beyond you?

It doesn't need to be. Being a bishop is very easy, if only you know how.

How is it possible? Well, really, there's a method that's right at your fingertips. And it's almost two thousand years old.

Jesus didn't start out with a Church under him. What he did instead was start with twelve disciples, who in turn discipled others. When he set the ball in motion, it grew and grew and grew.

Would you like to be a bishop? Let me explain how it's done. Then you'll see how many people you can have under you. All you have to do is edit the following list, then send it out to twelve people and the contact person at the bottom of the list. That's it! See, you have a list:

Write your name and email in the slot immediately above your rank, pushing others down to make room. For instance, if you're a layman, you put your name in the 'reader' slot, push everyone down, making the 'bishop' the 'contact bishop' below the list.

Then send the updated list to the new contact bishop, who will make arrangements for tonsures, ordinations, and consecrations.

Reader: Lawrence Town, lite@fastmail.fm
Subdeacon: Sdn. John Clough, jfc92847@aol.com
Deacon: Fr. Dn. John Cloud, john@johncloud.com
Priest: Fr. Andrew Costello, costello@pobox.com
Bishop: His Grace ANTHYMUS, anthymus@auth.gr
Contact Bishop (for tonsures/ordinations/consecrations): THOMAS, orthodoxthomas@x.com
Needs monastic tonsure (check one): [ ] Yes / [ ] No.

That's it! What happens now is that you will have twelve people below you, and if each of them has twelve people below them, then the number of people will shoot up, growing at a geometric rate like an intelligent computer in a bad science fiction movie! Just look at this chart, if you're a layman now, and I say *now*, because you don't need to be a layman for long!

Your Rank	Followers
Reader	12
Subdeacon	156
Deacon	1,884
Priest	22,620
Bishop	271,452

That's more than a quarter of a million followers when you're a bishop! And best of all, the opportunity doesn't stop there. As your own followers become deacons and then priests, you become an archbishop and a metropolitan. The sky is the limit!

It really works! I was a layman who found out this opportunity only three weeks ago, and now I'm His All Holiness

THOMAS, The Patriarch of Xanadu! Think about it! All you have to do is a little editing, and then forward this email! Can you afford to wait?

Do it now!

Cordially Yours,
X His All Holiness THOMAS, the Patriarch of Xanadu

Athanasius: *On Creative Fidelity*

Translator's Introduction

In an era of political correctness, it is always refreshing to discover a new manuscript from Athanasius, a saint a bit like gentle Jesus, meek and mild, who told the community's most respected members that they crossed land and sea to gain one single convert only to make this convert twice as much a child of Hell as they were themselves (Matt 23:15). In an era of political correctness, Athanasius can be a breath of fresh air.

In this hitherto undiscovered and unknown work, Athanasius addresses a certain (somewhat strange and difficult to understand) era's idiosyncracy in its adulation of what is termed "creative fidelity." His own era seems to be saying something to what that other era says about his era.

Athanasius: *On Creative Fidelity*

What is this madness I hear about "*creative fidelity*"? For it is actually reported to me that whenever one of you talks about being faithful to tradition, his first act is to parrot mad words about how "Being Orthodox has never been a matter of mindless parrot-like repetition of the past, but always a matter of creative fidelity."? *What madness is this?*

Is creative fidelity the fundamental truth about how to be an Orthodox Christian? Then why do we only hear about this at a time when people love innovation, when the madness of too many innovators to mention poisons the air as effectively as the heretic, the Antichrist, Arius? How is it that the Fathers, who are also alleged to participate in this diabolical "creative fidelity", did not understand what they were doing, but instead insisted in one and the same faith shared by the Church since its beginning? Is this because you understand the Fathers better than the Fathers themselves?

Is the report of blasphemy also true, that to conform to people's itching ears (II Tim 4:3) you shy back from the divine oracle, "But I want you to understand that the head of every man is Christ, the head of a woman is her husband, and the head of Christ is God." (I Cor 11:3)? There is something the Apostle so much wants you to understand, and perhaps if you understood it better you would not go so far astray as to seek the living among the dead (Luke 24:5) in your quest for creative fidelity.

How is it that you seek the living among the dead (Luke 24:5)? Christ is the head of the Church (Eph 5:23), of every man (I Cor 11:3), of every authority (Col 2:10), of all things (Eph 1:22,) and God is the head of Christ (I Cor 11:3). Christ is the one head, and because of him there are many heads. The sanctuary is the head of the nave: the place where sacred priests minister meets its glory and manifest interpretation (for as the divine Disciple tells us, the Son has interpreted the Father (John 1:18) to the world) in the nave where the brethren worship. The archetype is the head of the image, the saint the head of his icon, and indeed Heaven is the head of earth. And it is the head whose glory is manifest in the body.

If both incorruptible and unchangeable Heaven is the head of corruptible and changeable earth and yet earth manifests Heaven, what does this say about this strange thing you laud called "creative fidelity"? Does it not say something most disturbing? Does the one and the same faith, alive from the days of the apostles, belong to the corruptible or the incorruptible? Is it not unchangeable?

What then of those adaptations you make--even if some are good and some are even necessary? Do they not belong to the realm of the changeable and the realm of the corruptible?

Which then is to be head? Is the corruptible and changeable to be the head of the incorruptible that suffers no change? Or rather is not the heavenly incorruptible faith to be made manifest and interpreted in the world of change? Such creative fidelity as there may be cannot be the head, and when it usurps the place of the head, you make Heaven conform to earth. Such a people as yours is very good at making Heaven conform to earth!

Listen to me. When you prepare for the sacred Pascha, how many fasts are there? One of you fasts most strictly; another is too weak to fast; another has an observance somewhere between these poles, so that there are several ways of observing the fast.

Are there therefore many fasts? Are there many Lords (I Cor 8:5) honored when you fast? Or is it not one and the same fast which one observes according to the strictest letter, another with more accommodation, and each to the glory of God? Now which is the head, the variation in fasting, or the fast itself? Are the differences in observance the spiritual truth about the fast, or the one fast to the glory of the One Lord? Or do you think that because the fast may be relaxed in its observance, the most important truth is how many ways it may legitimately be observed?

So then, as the Church's fast is the head of the brethren's fast, be it strict or not strict, and it is one fast in the whole Church, so also there is one faith from the days of the Apostles. This I say not because I cannot notice the differences between the Fathers, but because these differences are not the head. The one fast is the head of various observances and the one faith perfectly delivered is the head even of creative fidelity, which has always appeared when people pursue the one faith and which has no need of our exhortations. Have the Fathers shown creative fidelity when they sought to preserve the one faith? If you say so, what does that say about your exhortation to creative fidelity? Is it needed? Do you also exhort people to wrong others so that the flower of forgiveness may show forth? Or is there not enough opportunity for the flower of forgiveness without seeking it out? Show creative fidelity when you must, but must you seek it out? Must you make it the head? Must you make the Fathers wrong when they lay a foundation, not of each day's idiosyncracies in being faithful, but in the one faith that like Heaven cannot suffer change and like Heaven is what should be made manifest in earth?

Why do you seek the living among the dead (Luke 24:5)? Our confession has a great High Priest (Heb 3:1) who has passed through the Heavens (Heb 4:14) to that Temple and Tradition, that Sanctuary, of which every changeable earthen tradition is merely a shadow and a copy (Heb 8:5) and which the saints of the ages are ever more fully drawn to participate! Therefore, since we are surrounded by such a great cloud of witnesses and the Great Witness himself, let us also lay aside every weight, and change, and sin which so easily entangles, and run with perseverance the race that is set before us (Heb 12:1), changing that we may leave change behind!

Remember that you are not walking, as you say, the Orthodox System of Concepts, but the Orthodox Way. Remember that feeding the hungry (**Matthew 25:35**); is greater than raising the dead. Never let the lamp of your prayers go out (**I Thess 5:17**. Like the Father, be a father to the fatherless (**Ps 68:5**; **Isa 1:17**). All the brethren salute you (**Rom 16:16**; **II Cor 13:13**). Greet one another with a holy kiss (**Rom 16:16**; **I Cor 16:20**; **II Cor 13:2**; **I Thess 5:26**; **I Pet 5:11**).

On Mentorship

The specific principles which I see as applicable to mentorship are as follows:

- Love is the foundation to all healthy human relationships. The mentoring relationship is first and foremost a human relationship, and will function best if it is a relationship between whole persons built on love and friendship.
- Effective teaching in that context begins, not with the mentor talking, but listening. There are at least three reasons for this:
- Listening is valuable in and of itself.
- When a person is listened to, it helps him to trust and open up. This will help the teacher to gain a very important trust in instructing the student.
- It will give the mentor a basis to connect with the student, and tailor messages to him.
- Beauty is forged in the eye of the beholder. A willing student can be powerfully shaped by a mentor who looks at him and sees him, not merely as he is, but as he will become.

- Effective mentoring is not only teaching of one specific area, but first and foremost a teaching about life. It is teaching of life and wisdom in such a way as to usually take the form of a kind of specific lesson.
- The mentor should approach the relationship as being for the student's benefit, and only incidentally for his own. He should be willing to do things that are difficult for him, and he should be happy for the student's success -- even (especially) when the student does better than him, or catches him in error.
- The mentor should not only be concerned with imparting knowledge, but more importantly concerned with helping the student to think and use knowledge effectively.
- The mentor should not be trying to clone himself or make the student an extension of himself. He should try to help the student be the person God created him to be, not who the mentor wants to be or in fantasy would selfishly like him to be.
- The student should not be passive, regarding the mentorship as something which is done to him. He should regard it as a resource to take advantage of in his efforts to actively learn. He should take responsibility on himself for his own progress. He should concentrate on actively listening, and asking intelligent questions. The student should be like Prometheus, looking for every opportunity to steal knowledge from his teacher.
- Both parties should work hard -- not asking "Can this work?", but "How will we make this work?" Persistent in making things work, the mentor should none the less vary his methods of explanation, like water flowing down a hill -- it *will* get around obstacles, and it does so by flowing around and through them, which is in turn accomplished by adapting its shape to whatever there is, and thereby

slipping around obstacles that would stop a rolling rock.

[N.B. The following segment refers to the following joke/story, recounted in Reader's Digest:

A professor believed that his students were mindlessly copying too much of his lectures instead of thinking and then writing down key points. One day in class, he interrupted his lecture and said, "Stop. I want you to put down your pens and pencils and listen to me. You are not here to transcribe my lectures. You are here to think first and foremost, and only then to write down the essence of what I am saying. You don't have to write down every word I say verbatim. Now, any questions?"

One student raised her hand. "Yes?" "How do you spell 'verbatim'?"]

- A rare but important part of teaching is shattering limits on the way a person is thinking ("How do you spell 'verbatim'?"). This should never be done lightly or as a first approach, nor should it be done carelessly or insensitively. It needs to be done with the utmost care, and is probably very difficult to do well. That stated, a mentor does a student no service by helping him to write down an hour's worth of requests to stop writing and start thinking.
- Metacognitive thought is important both for mentor and apprentice. The mentor should be thinking about both his own thought and the student's, and when the student isn't hearing what the mentor is saying, the mentor should ask, "How am I thinking? How is he thinking? Why are we not connecting?" -- but he should primarily be concerned for the student's thought. The student should be thinking about both people's thought as well -- the mentor's, because it is an example of how an expert thinks, and his own, because if he understands how he is thinking he will be better prepared to transcend his current limits. Both of them should expect the other to periodically have an alien

insight to share that won't fit in their present mindsets.

- The mentor should be emotionally intelligent, and be sensitive to the emotions and emotional needs of the student. If the student is not in the right emotional state, learning will be almost impossible. We are not just pure, emotionless minds, and we can be far more effective if we care for emotions and use them then if we act as if emotions were not a serious part of us. If either person is not able to give full attention, a meeting should be either shortened or postponed.
- The mentor, precisely because he is a unique leader, should take the attitude of a servant to the student, just as Jesus washed his disciples' feet.
- The mentor should realize that the lesson he is teaching is first, who he is; second, what he does; third, what he says. The mentor should model an excitement and interest in the material, and focus less on what to think than how to think. He should also model before the student effective human relationships with other people.
- In the beginning especially, the mentor should not deluge the apprentice with information. Assimilating new and foreign information -- particularly when you don't have a framework to put things into -- is hard, and overloading a student prevents him from learning anything. A mentor should begin by asking questions of the student, trying to understand him better, and only slowly ease into talking about philosophical frameworks and then details of the subject area of the mentoring.
- The mentor and eventually the student should know not only their cognitive strengths, but at least as importantly their cognitive weaknesses -- both those that are part of being human, and those that are specific to a person. Code Complete (referenced below) says that there is a tenfold

productivity difference made when programmers use principles and techniques grounded in a respect for cognitive weaknesses.

- The mentor should be an expert in his field, and should also be continuing to learn and do research. Graduation is not the end of learning, but a beginning of a new kind of learning.

- The mentor should help the student to put the day's lessons into practice. The student should be asking the question, "How can I apply this? How can I practice it?" Homework will help the student to learn, although perhaps shouldn't be started until the mentor has earned the student's trust and the student is motivated to use homework assignments to squeeze every last benefit out of time with the mentor.

- The student should be safe and free to make mistakes, for a couple of reasons. First, if he isn't making at least some mistakes, he probably isn't being challenged enough or learning enough new material. Second, a mistake is a tremendous educational opportunity. It provides a unique insight into the student's thought, and therefore should be treasured, grasped, analyzed.

- There is no quick fix. The most effective (and, for that matter, even the fastest) way to get results is to work slowly, patiently, unhurriedly towards achieving mastery. There is often a tradeoff between optimizing for short term and long term effectiveness; patiently working for long term payoffs will ultimately produce the highest dividends.

I will also mention several books which provide a backdrop to my comments, three that I would strongly reccommend and four that I would suggest:

Strongly Recommended:

- The Bible. That has provided the theological and philosophical grounding to my thought as a whole; it gives the structure/meta-structure which I fit the other points into. (This is the most important, but it is not necessary to read cover to cover before beginning anything. Fifteen or thirty minutes a day will add up to a lot if continued for a couple years.) Particularly relevant passages that come to mind are Matthew 5-7 (the Sermon on the Mount), I Cor. 13 (the hymn to love), much of the Johannine writings (esp. John 13-17), and certain areas of Proverbs.
- *Seven Habits of Highly Effective People*. A classic.
- *How to Win Friends and Influence People*. Although much of the influence it deals with is persuasive in character, the same principles apply to the kind of influence necessary to effectively mentor.

Suggested:

- *Listening, A Practical Approach*. Probably one among many books on listening, this deals with an extremely valuable and neglected area of communication.
- *Emotional Intelligence*. We are not pure minds, and we can cripple ourselves terribly if we do not handle our emotions effectively. If we do, they will help us greatly.
- *Code Complete: A Practical Handbook of Software Construction*. In computer science, most of the programming materials talk about how to effectively use computers, taking advantage of their strengths and dealing with their weaknesses, to get a computer to do something. This book talks about how to effectively use your mind,

taking advantage of its strengths and dealing with its weaknesses, to get a computer to do something. The kind of thinking involved is applicable far beyond computer science.

- Gandhi's writings. I could mention specific chapters in what I've read, but I will say that there is a general theme of spiritual force instead of physical force, and the spiritual force which he advocates (which helped him to turn bitter enemies into warm friends) has tremendous relevance to mentorship. In *Autobiographical Reflections*, in a chapter entitled "Ahimse or the way of nonviolence", he comments that when a parent slaps a child, what affects the child is not so much the sting of the slap, as the offended love which lies behind that slap.

Halloween

A Solemn Farewell

I remember, from when I was a little boy, that I asked my parents some question about Halloween, and I was told that I would be welcome to dress up, but not as something occult or macabre, like a witch or a zombie. My Mom helped me put together several homemade costumes, and my parents accompanied me for years of trick-or-treating. I was, in essence, invited to celebrate Halloween as a secular holiday (in time, it became my second favorite holiday), but not to celebrate ghoulishness.

Some readers may see this as needless legalism about something harmless. A few Christians who have concerns about Halloween might wonder if I was being invited to participate in something un-Christian. But back in the eighties, where it was considered superstition to believe that witches really existed, my parents took seriously something that more people take seriously today: not everything about Halloween is trivial or absolutely harmless.

In retrospect, I am quite grateful for this decision, and I respect it, much as I appreciate their decision to limit my time watching television, while encouraging me to play outside, read books, and tinker with mechanical things. (I do not own a television now, and I am glad not to have one.)

Not, in particular, that I feel any guilt about dressing up as my favorite TV character (MacGyver), or creating homemade costumes, one of which won an award. But there seemed to be, if not absolute innocence, at least a grey area. There are many things I disagreed (and disagree) with my parents about, but I really saw no need to reconsider what my parents taught me here. Even if I was trying to smoke Halloween without inhaling anything macabre, there seemed to be a reasonable case for this attempt to "smoke, but not inhale." I believed that I was succeeding in taking Halloween *à la carte* and dressing up without participating in anything either my parents or I would have objected to.

But something has changed. Even though it has again become fashionable for adults (as well as children) to dress up as Halloween, I am finding that I have concerns about what exactly it is that is fashionable. It seemed to be the sort of thing you could least give the benefit of the doubt, but that seems a harder benefit to give now. There are other things going on in this occult awakening; I would like to look at herbs. Perhaps people have thought of herbs simply as a seasoning for cooks to use. This is no longer true. It is no longer enough to say that people also see herbs as a natural alternative to chemically manufactured medicines, even if that is no doubt true. Herbs are part of a picture that is changing with a magical awakening. Seeing ads for herbs for witches' use and growing witches' gardens is the tip of an iceberg. Herbs are microcosm of a picture that is changing.

Before I go on, let me be very clear about something, as I am going to be talking a fair bit about herbs.

There is an old Orthodox saying that talks about spending Church money: "If you have two small coins, you use one to buy bread for the offering, and you use the other to buy flowers for the altar." The point isn't really about herbs, but it is entirely appropriate that herbs come to mind even when making a point that isn't really about herbs. A great many of the holiest things in

Orthodoxy come from herbs: flowers to adorn the icons regularly, adorning the whole Church along with other herbs for the greatest festivities; herbal aromatic resins making incense; olive oil, mingled possibly with herbs, for every sacred anointing, wood as the most fitting material for icons, and bread and wine for the greatest and holiest rite there is. There is one rite labelled as the rite for the blessing of herbs, but herbs are blessed on a number of other occasions as well. Nature, including herbs, keeps coming up in the liturgy.

But you really cannot understand what this means until you come to the tale of herbs, if you remember that trees are herbs. I am thinking about two trees in particular.

One of these two trees was set in the center of a garden of unequalled splendor, and our first mother looked at its fruit with greedy spiritual lust, saw what the fruit could do, and then ate from it. She experienced a thrill of almost indescribable ecstasy, which quickly vanished into horror, despair, and misery. She had been created immortal, believed the words, "You shall be like gods," found that what was created godlike about her was slipping through her fingers, and felt the seed of death already working in her heart.

That is how our first mother fell. Her husband did no better, and Orthodox writers blame now one, now the other, but I am interested in something besides assigning blame.

That is not the last tree to bear fruit, nor is it the end of the story. The wound that came by the first tree had its answer and healing from the second tree. First there was a new Eve, who triumphed where the first had failed. Then the new Adam, fully God, fully man, whose life was a journey to not a living tree in paradise but a dead tree in a desolate place: for the Cross has been considered a tree from ancient times. But this last tree is ultimately transfigured to be the Tree of Life. We were forbidden to eat from the first tree. But the Tree of Life has its own fruit, and we are commanded to eat from its fruit.

Every herb that is part of the Church's blessings is an outpouring of that last herb, the Cross. We can and should feed on herbs. But it matters a great deal *which* herb we are feeding on. And Halloween has the taste of the fruit of the first tree.

I am concerned about the history of Halloween, *up to a point*. It is said that various pagan customs in a fight against Christianity, are at the root of almost every Halloween custom we have today--Christianity was shaped by martyrs who chose to be killed rather than offer just a pinch of incense in pagan sacrifice, and some have said that people would intimidate Christians by threatening offensive acts of vandalism unless they gave them food to use in pagan sacrifice, and that when we say "Trick or treat," we are carrying on a custom that began with a rather vile form of extortion.

This explanation may or may not be true, and my first thought--perhaps not the most Orthodox thought--was, "The origin of something is not its present meaning." A standard illustration is that shaking hands is a custom from the far past that was originally to prevent another person from drawing a weapon--a bit like reaching for a can of pepper spray. As such, it is a poor candidate for a friendly greeting. But it really seems hard to believe that learning something like this is a reason to try to avoid shaking hands. And the fact that a particular practice has an origins Christians today might find vile is not decisive by itself. Even what those origins were is hard to tell, as the historical data are incomplete and highly ambiguous.

But there is another concern. Let's set aside murky questions about where Halloween comes from. There is the question of what Halloween is *now*, which is far less murky on several counts. Whatever the good, bad, known, or unknown roots of Halloween may be, in its present form it is associated with magic or ghoulishness--you're not barred from dressing up as something that is neither associated with the occult or ghoulishness, but you're stretching things a little. That much was true in my childhood. What was not true in my childhood is that Halloween is quickly becoming a second national holiday. When I was growing up, you could buy or rent costumes, but now there seem to be large, heavily-funded Halloween stores. There were yard decorations--not just pumpkins--during my childhood, and I remember putting up a package of imitation spider web. Today there are, as before Christmas, large and elaborate yard displays that are much more impressive than a snowman. But gone are the days when my parents seemed quaint for saying that magic is real and to be avoided, or just for taking magic seriously. Even a skeptic would need to be trying to be obtuse to deny that a lot of people are trying to be magicians of some sort.

I am grateful to my parents for giving Halloween the benefit of the doubt. There was really something special to me. But I am coming to a point of saying that appearances do not always deceive, and that a festival celebrating the spooky, a festival to dress up as zombies and witches and decorate with the macabre, and so on may in fact be a spiritual force, an appetizer, if you will, for the herb that gave our race the seed of death.

If one is trying to make an Orthodox response to Halloween, there is one obvious response of keeping out of the holiday and praying. Another Orthodox response to Halloween has been to have a parish party for all the children, inviting them to dress up as their patron saints. This decision may sound like a shallow change, but it shows wisdom and theological beauty. Trying to be like your patron saint is not just a day's make-believe, but a lifelong imitation and challenge. Your patron saint is to look out for you, praying before God. This adaptation is well-chosen, and is in the spirit of the original intent: "Halloween" abbreviates "Hallowe'en", "All Hallows Eve", the evening of all hallowed people, holy people, an evening that was in fact the beginning of All Saints' Day. And perhaps there are others.

But perhaps the best response Orthodoxy is not obvious if you are trying to think of something to do.

The spiritual world, in Orthodoxy, is never really far; we can be insensitive to it but never escape it. Orthodoxy provides not a single holiday each year but unfolding seasons and cycles of spiritual discipline and life as they encounter all kinds of spiritual realities. (Many people look for the spirit world to be closer at

Halloween.) Death is important in Orthodoxy. Orthodoxy is a mystery of life in death, and to fail to be mindful of death is a profound spiritual failure. Even if Halloween eclipses Christmas, the Orthodox concern is not that people are too interested in death, but that people are not engaging death enough, and the ways we are engaging death are not nearly deep enough. Nor is the line in the living and the dead within the Church any terribly great chasm. But although these things are present in the Orthodox Church--woven into its fabric--they all rest in the protecting shade of the Tree of Life, and it is a protection that they all need. The concern is not at all that people are getting interested in spiritual phenomena, but that they are pursuing that interest in the wrong way, tasting from the herb that is poison when they could be eating their fill from the herb that is life and medicine and healing. It is a "treasure hunting" that consists of digging around to find a few copper coins hidden in a dark place... when there are piles of gold out in the open.

If Jack'o'lanterns have the origin I have heard, then they are not a pagan custom, at least not in the sense that Druids used them in worship. The candle is of Christian origin, and more specifically, made to be a frightening mockery of the candles in Christian worship. In Orthodoxy today, beeswax candles still illuminate icons, which have a spiritual radiance shining through. (Heaven shines out through them.) They can take time to connect with, but people can look at them and continue to see something for years. I would have trouble finding new layers in a Jack'o'lantern over years, and not only because they would go bad. It's not as deep a kind of thing. The difference between the two is like the difference between one of Bach's fugues, and Bart Simpson butchering an advertising jingle.

I do plan on dressing up for Halloween one last time. Call it, if nothing else, a farewell, in addition to some more mundane reasons. It has been a cherished holiday for years. But only in the shallowest sense am I saying farewell to what I most valued about Halloween.

At Vespers, we chant, "The Lord is King; he has put on

majesty." This "put on" is a translation of a Greek word, *enduno* (ενδυνο), a word of being equipped. The Epistle to the Ephesians tells us to "put on" full Heavenly armor that includes the breastplate of righteousness and the helmet of salvation. In Isaiah, it is God who puts on the breastplate of righteousness and the helmet of salvation for spiritual war. Not to put too fine a point it, but we have a command to put on God's own armor, and that is not all. At baptism, one of the most memorable parts is the verse chanted from Scripture, "As many as have been baptized in Christ, have put on Christ."

At an ordination, the ordinand is clothed in liturgical vestments that remain almost unchanged since Byzantine times when they were court regalia. But this is not a costume that people pretend for a day. The person is made into something new, and when the ordinand puts on the garments, he puts on a new blessing and sacred service. But it is a fundamental mistake to think that royal priesthood is only for those who are ordained and "wear vestments": the bishop is called to put on the regalia of the Byzantine Emperor, but the whole Church is called to put on Christ. This is no mere costume but a transformation of the highest order.

Perhaps we need to give up our Halloween costumes, to make room to put on something far greater: Christ himself. But that is not simply something to do about Halloween: it is the work of a lifetime and it includes the entirety of Christian practice. (Even if it might be a good idea to simply pray over Halloween.)

A Pet Owner's Rules

God is a pet owner who has two rules, and only two rules. They are:

1. I am your owner. Enjoy freely the food and water which I have provided for your good!
2. Don't drink out of the toilet.

That's really it. Those are the only two rules we are expected to follow. And we still break them.

Drunkenness is drinking out of the toilet. If you ask most recovering alcoholics if the time they were drunk all the time were their most joyful, merry, halcyon days, I don't know exactly how they'd answer, if they could even keep a straight face. Far from being joyful, being drunk all the time is misery that most recovering alcoholics wouldn't wish on their worst enemies. If you are drunk all the time, you lose the ability to enjoy much of anything. Strange as it may sound, it takes sobriety to enjoy even drunkenness. Drunkenness is drinking out of the toilet.

Lust is also drinking out of the toilet. Lust is the disenchantment of the entire universe. It is a magic spell where suddenly nothing else is interesting, and after lust destroys the ability to enjoy anything else, lust destroys the ability to enjoy even lust. Proverbs says, "The adulterous woman"--today one might add, "and internet pornography" to that--"in the beginning is as sweet as honey and in the end as bitter as gall and as sharp as a double-edged sword." Now this is talking about a lot more than pleasure, but it is talking about pleasure. Lust, a sin of pleasure, ends by destroying pleasure. It takes chastity to enjoy even lust.

Having said that lust is drinking out of the toilet, I'd like to clarify something. There are eight particularly dangerous sins the Church warns us about. That's one, and it isn't the most serious. Sins of lust are among the most easily forgiven; the Church's most scathing condemnations go to sins like pride and running the poverty industry. The harshest condemnations go to sins that are deliberate, cold-blooded sins, not so much disreputable, hot-blooded sins like lust. Lust is drinking out of the toilet, but there are much worse problems.

I'd like you to think about the last time you traveled from one place to another and you enjoyed the scenery. That's good, and it's something that greed destroys. Greed destroys the ability to enjoy things without needing to own them, and there are a lot of things in life (like scenery) that we can enjoy if we are able to enjoy things without always having to make them mine, mine, mine. Greed isn't about enjoying things; it's about grasping and letting the ability to enjoy things slip through your fingers. When people aren't greedy, they know contentment; they can enjoy their own things without wishing they were snazzier or newer or more antique or what have you. (And if you do get that hot possession you've been coveting, greed destroys the ability to simply enjoy it: it becomes as dull and despicable as all your possessions look when you look at them through greed's darkened eyes. It takes contentment to enjoy even greed: greed is *also* drinking out of the toilet.

Jesus had some rather harsh words after being unforgiving after God has forgiven us so much. Even though forgiveness is work, refusing to forgive one other person is drinking out of the toilet. Someone said it's like drinking poison and hoping it will hurt the other person.

The last sin I'll mention is pride, even though *all* sin is drinking out of the toilet. Pride is not about joy; pride destroys joy. Humility is less about pushing yourself down than an attitude that lets you respect and enjoy others. Pride makes people sneer at others who they can only see as despicable, and when you can't enjoy anyone else, you are too poisoned to enjoy yourself. If you catch yourself enjoying pride, repent of it, but if you can enjoy pride at all, you haven't hit rock bottom. As G.K. Chesterton said, it takes humility to enjoy even pride. Pride is drinking out of the toilet. *All* sin is drinking out of the toilet.

I've talked about drinking out of the toilet, but Rule Number Two is not the focus. Rule Number One is, "I am your owner. Enjoy freely of the food and water I have given you." Rule Number Two, "Don't drink out of the toilet," is only important when we break it, which is unfortunately quite a lot. The second rule is really a footnote meant to help us focus on Rule Number One, the real rule.

What is Rule Number One about? One window that lets us glimpse the beauty of Rule Number One is, "If you have faith the size of a mustard seed, you can say to a mountain, 'Be uprooted and thrown into the sea,' and it will be done for you." Is this exaggeration? Yes. More specifically, it's the kind of exaggeration the Bible uses to emphasize important points. Being human sometimes means that there are mountains that are causing us real trouble. If someone remains in drunkenness and becomes an alcoholic, that alcoholism becomes a mountain that no human strength is strong enough to move. I've known several Christians who were recovering alcoholics. And had been sober for years. *That* is a mountain moved by faith. Without exception, they have become some of the most Christlike, loving people I have known. That is what can happen when we receive freely of the food and drink our Lord provides us. And it's not the only example. There has been an Orthodox resurrection in Albania. Not long ago, it was a church in ruins as part of a country that was ruins. Now the Albanian Orthodox Church is alive and strong, and a powerhouse of transformation for the whole nation. God is on the move in Albania. He's moved mountains.

To eat of the food and drink the Lord has provided--and, leaving the image of dog food behind, this means not only the Eucharist but the whole life God provides--makes us share in the divine nature and live the divine life. We can bring Heaven down to earth, not only beginning ourselves to live the heavenly life, but beginning to establish Heaven around us through our good works. It means that we share in good things we don't always know to ask.

Let's choose the food and drink we were given.

A Wonderful Life

Peter never imagined that smashing his thumb in a car door would be the best thing to ever happened to him. But suddenly his plans to move in to the dorm were changed, and he waited a long time at the hospital before finally returning to the dorm and moving in.

Peter arrived for the second time well after check-in time, praying to be able to get in. After a few phone calls, a security officer came in, expressed sympathy about his bandaged thumb, and let him up to his room. The family moved his possessions from the car to his room and made his bed in a few minutes, and by the time it was down, the security guard had called the RA, who brought Peter his keys.

It was the wee hours of the morning when Peter looked at his new home for the second time, and tough as Peter was, the pain in his thumb kept him from falling asleep. He was in as much pain as he'd been in for a while.

He awoke when the light was ebbing, and after some preparations set out, wandering until he found the cafeteria. The pain seemed much when he sat down at a table. (It took him a while to find a seat because the cafeteria was crowded.)

A young man said, "Hi, I'm John." Peter began to extend his hand, then looked at his white bandaged thumb and said, "Excuse me for not shaking your hand. I am Peter."

A young woman said, "I'm Mary. I saw you earlier and was hoping to see you more."

Peter wondered about something, then said, "I'll drink for that," reached with his right hand, grabbed a glass of soda, and then winced in pain, spilling his drink on the table.

Everybody at the table moved. A couple of people dodged the flow of liquid; others stopped what they were doing, rushing to mop up the spill with napkins. Peter said, "I keep forgetting I need to be careful about my thumb," smiled, grabbed his glass of milk, and slipped again, spilling milk all over his food.

Peter stopped, sat back, and then laughed for a while. "This is an interesting beginning to my college education."

Mary said, "I noticed you managed to smash your thumb in a car door without saying any words you regret. What else has happened?"

Peter said, "Nothing great; I had to go to the ER, where I had to wait, before they could do something about my throbbing thumb. I got back at 4:00 AM and couldn't get to sleep for a long time because I was in so much pain. Then I overslept my alarm and woke up naturally in time for dinner. How about you?"

Mary thought for a second about the people she met. Peter could see the sympathy on her face.

John said, "Wow. That's nasty."

Peter said, "I wish we couldn't feel pain. Have you thought about how nice it would be to live without pain?"

Mary said, "I'd like that."

John said, "Um..."

Mary said, "What?"

John said, "Actually, there are people who don't feel pain, and there's a name for the condition. You've heard of it."

Peter said, "I haven't heard of that before."

John said, "Yes you have. It's called leprosy."

Peter said, "What do you mean by 'leprosy'? I thought leprosy was a disease that ravaged the body."

John said, "It is. But that is only because it destroys the ability to feel pain. The way it works is very simple. We all get little nicks and scratches, and because they hurt, we show extra sensitivity. Our feet start to hurt after a long walk, so without even thinking about it we... shift things a little, and keep anything really bad from happening. That pain you are feeling is your body's way of asking room to heal so that the smashed thumbnail (or whatever it is) that hurts so terribly now won't leave you permanently maimed. Back to feet, a leprosy patient will walk exactly the same way and get wounds we'd never even think of for taking a long walk. All the terrible injuries that make leprosy a feared disease happen *only* because leprosy keeps people from feeling pain."

Peter looked at his thumb, and his stomach growled.

John said, "I'm full. Let me get a drink for you, and then I'll help you drink it."

Mary said, "And I'll get you some dry food. We've already eaten; it must--"

Peter said, "Please, I've survived much worse. It's just a bit of pain."

John picked up a clump of wet napkins and threatened to throw it at Peter before standing up and walking to get something to drink. Mary followed him.

Peter sat back and just laughed.

John said, "We have some time free after dinner; let's just wander around campus."

They left the glass roofed building and began walking around, enjoying the grass and the scenery.

After some wandering, Peter and those he had just met looked at the castle-like Blanchard Hall, each one transported in his imagination to be in a more ancient era, and walked around the campus, looked at a fountain, listened to some music, and looked at a display of a giant mastodon which had died before the end of the last ice age, and whose bones had been unearthed in a nearby excavation. They got lost, but this was not a terrible concern; they were taking in the campus.

Their slow walk was interrupted when John looked at his watch and realized it was time for the "floor fellowship." and orientation games.

Between orientation games, Peter heard bits of conversation: "This has been a bummer; I've gotten two papercuts this week." "--and then I--" "What instruments do you--" "I'm from France too! *Tu viens de Paris?*" "Really? You--" Everybody seemed to be chattering, and Peter wished he could be in one of--actually, several of those conversations at once.

Paul's voice cut in and said, "For this next activity we are going to form a human circle. With your team, stand in a circle, and everybody reach in and grab another hand with each hand. Then hold on tight; when I say, "Go," you want to untangle yourselves, without letting go. The first team to untangle themselves wins!"

Peter reached in, and found each of his hands clasped in a solid, masculine grip. Then the race began, and people jostled and tried to untangle themselves. This was a laborious process and, one by one, every other group freed itself, while Peter's group seemed stuck on--someone called and said, "I think we're knotted!" As people began to thin out, Paul looked with astonishment and saw that they were indeed knotted. "A special prize to them, too, for managing the best tangle!"

"And now, we'll have a three-legged race! Gather into pairs, and each two of you take a burlap sack. Then--" Paul continued, and with every game, the talk seemed to flow more. When the finale finished, Peter found himself again with John and Mary and heard the conversations flowing around him: "Really? You too?" "But you don't understand. Hicks have a slower pace of life; we enjoy things without all the things you city dwellers need for entertainment. And we learn resourceful ways to--" "--and only at Wheaton would the administration *forbid* dancing while *requiring* the games we just played and--" Then Peter lost himself in a conversation that continued long into the night. He expected to be up at night thinking about all the beloved people he left at home, but Peter was too busy thinking about John's and Mary's stories.

The next day Peter woke up his to the hideous sound of his alarm clock, and groggily trudged to the dining hall for coffee, and searched for his advisor.

Peter found the appropriate hallway, wandered around nervously until he found a door with a yellowed plaque that said "Julian Johnson," knocked once, and pushed the door open. A white-haired man said, "Peter Jones? How are you? Do come in... What can I do for you?"

Peter pulled out a sheet of paper, looked down at it for a moment and said, "I'm sorry I'm late. I need you to write what courses I should take and sign here. Then I can be out of your way."

The old man sat back, drew a deep breath, and relaxed into a fatherly smile. Peter began to wonder if his advisor was going to say anything at all. Then Prof. Johnson motioned towards an armchair, as rich and luxurious as his own, and then looked as if he remembered something and offered a bowl full of candy. "Sit down, sit down, and make yourself comfortable. May I interest you in candy?" He picked up an engraved metal bowl and held it out while Peter grabbed a few Lifesavers.

Prof. Johnson sat back, silent for a moment, and said, "I'm sorry I'm out of butterscotch; that always seems to disappear. Please sit down, and tell me about yourself. We can get to that form in a minute. One of the priveleges of this job is that I get to meet interesting people. Now, where are you from?"

Peter said, "I'm afraid there's not much that's interesting about me. I'm from a small town downstate that doesn't have anything to distinguish itself. My amusements have been reading, watching the cycle of the year, oh, and running. Not much interesting in that. Now which classes should I take?"

Prof. Johnson sat back and smiled, and Peter became a little less tense. "You run?"

Peter said, "Yes; I was hoping to run on the track this afternoon, after the lecture. I've always wanted to run on a real track."

The old man said, "You know, I used to run myself, before I became an official Old Geezer and my orthopaedist told me my knees couldn't take it. So I have to content myself with swimming now, which I've grown to love. Do you know about the Prairie Path?"

Peter said, "No, what's that?"

Prof. Johnson said, "Years ago, when I ran, I ran through the areas surrounding the College--there are a lot of beautiful houses. And, just south of the train tracks with the train you can hear now, there's a path before you even hit the street. You can run, or bike, or walk, on a path covered with fine white gravel, with trees and prairie plants on either side. It's a lovely view." He paused, and said, "Any ideas what you want to do after Wheaton?"

Peter said, "No. I don't even know what I want to major in."

Prof. Johnson said, "A lot of students don't know what they want to do. Are you familiar with Career Services? They can help you get an idea of what kinds of things you like to do."

Peter looked at his watch and said, "It's chapel time."

Prof. Johnson said, "Relax. I can write you a note." Peter began to relax again, and Prof. Johnson continued, "Now you like to read. What do you like to read?"

Peter said, "Newspapers and magazines, and I read this really cool book called *Zen and the Art of Motorcycle Maintenance.* Oh, and I like the Bible."

Prof. Johnson said, "I do too. What do you like about it most?"

"I like the stories in the Old Testament."

"One general tip: here at Wheaton, we have different kinds of professors--"

Peter said, "Which ones are best?"

Prof. Johnson said, "Different professors are best for different students. Throughout your tenure at Wheaton, ask your friends and learn which professors have teaching styles that you learn well with and mesh well with. Consider taking other courses from a professor you like. Now we have a lot of courses which we think expose you to new things and stretch you--people come back and see that these courses are best. Do you like science?"

"I like it; I especially liked a physics lab."

Prof. Johnson began to flip through the course catalogue. "Have you had calculus?" Prof. Johnson's mind wandered over the differences between from the grand, Utopian vision for "calculus" as it was first imagined and how different a conception it had from anything that would be considered "mathematics" today. Or should he go into that? He wavered, and then realized Peter had answered his question. "Ok," Prof. Johnson said, "the lab physics class unfortunately requires that you've had calculus. Would you like to take calculus now? Have you had geometry, algebra, and trigonometry?"

Peter said, "Yes, I did, but I'd like a little break from that now. Maybe I could take calculus next semester."

"Fair enough. You said you liked to read."

"Magazines and newspapers."

"Those things deal with the unfolding human story. I wonder if you'd like to take world civilization now, or a political science course."

"History, but why study world history? Why can't I just study U.S. history?"

Prof. Johnson said, "The story of our country is intertwined with that of our world. I think you might find that some of the things in world history are a lot closer to home than you think--and we have some real storytellers in our history department."

"That sounds interesting. What else?"

"The Theology of Culture class is one many students find enjoyable, and it helps build a foundation for Old and New Testament courses. Would you be interested in taking it for A quad or B quad, the first or second half of the semester?"

"Could I do both?"

"I wish I could say yes, but this course only lasts half the semester. The other half you could take Foundations of Wellness--you could do running as homework!"

"I think I'll do that first, and then Theology of Culture. That should be new," Peter said, oblivious to how tightly connected he was to theology and culture. "What else?"

Prof. Johnson said, "We have classes where people read

things that a lot of people have found really interesting. Well, that could describe several classes, but I was thinking about Classics of Western Literature or Literature of the Modern World."

Peter said, "Um... Does Classics of Western Literature cover ancient and medieval literature, and Literature of the Modern World cover literature that isn't Western? Because if they do, I'm not sure I could connect with it."

Prof. Johnson relaxed into his seat. "You know, a lot of people think that. But you know what?"

Peter said, "What?"

"There is something human that crosses cultures. That is why the stories have been selected. Stories written long ago, and stories written far away, can have a lot to connect with."

"Ok. How many more courses should I take?"

"You're at 11 credits now; you probably want 15. Now you said that you like *Zen and the Art of Motorcycle Maintenance*. I'm wondering if you would also like a philosophy course."

Peter said, "*Zen and the Art of Motorcycle Maintenance* is... I don't suppose there are any classes that use that. Or are there? I've heard Pirsig isn't given his fair due by philosophers."

Prof. Johnson said, "If you approach one of our philosophy courses the way you approach *Zen and the Art of Motorcycle Maintenance*, I think you'll profit from the encounter. I wonder if our Issues and Worldviews in Philosophy might interest you. I'm a big fan of thinking worldviewishly, and our philosophers have some pretty interesting things to say."

Peter asked, "What does 'worldviewishly' mean?"

Prof. Johnson searched for an appropriate simplification. "It means thinking in terms of worldviews. A worldview is the basic philosophical framework that gives shape to how we view the world. Our philosophers will be able to help you understand the basic issues surrounding worldviews and craft your own Christian worldview. You may find this frees you from the Enlightenment's secularizing influence--and if you don't know what the Enlightenment is now, you will learn to understand it, and its problems, and how you can be somewhat freer of its chain."

Peter said, "Ok. Well, I'll take those classes. It was good to meet you."

Prof. Johnson looked at the class schedule and helped Peter choose class sections, then said, "I enjoyed talking with you. Please do take some more candy--put a handful in your pocket or something. I just want to make one more closing comment. I want to see you succeed. Wheaton wants to see you succeed. There are some rough points and problems along the way, and if you bring them to me I can work with them and try to help you. If you want to talk with your RA or our chaplain or someone else, that's fine, but please... my door is *always* open. And it was good to meet you too! Goodbye!"

Peter walked out, completely relaxed, and was soon to be energized in a scavenger hunt searching for things from a dog biscuit to a car bumper to a burning sheet of paper not lit by someone in his group, before again relaxing into the "brother-sister floor fellowship" which combined mediocre "7-11 praise songs" (so called because they have "7 words, repeated 11 times") with the light of another world shining through.

It was not long before the opening activities wound down and Peter began to settle into a regular routine.

Peter and Mary both loved to run, but for different reasons. Peter was training himself for various races; he had not joined track, as he did in high school, but there were other races. Mary ran to feel the sun and wind and rain. And, without any conscious effort, they found themselves running together down the prairie path together, and Peter clumsily learning to match his speed to hers. And, as time passed, they talked, and talked, and talked, and talked, and their runs grew longer.

When the fall break came, they both joined a group going to the northwoods of Wisconsin for a program that was half-work and half-play. And each one wrote a letter home about the other. Then Peter began his theology of culture class, and said, "This is what I want to study." Mary did not have a favorite class, at least not that she realized, until Peter asked her what her favorite class was and she said, "Literature."

When Christmas came, they went to their respective homes and spent the break thinking about each other, and they talked about this when they returned. They ended the conversation, or at least they thought they did, and then each hurried back to catch the other and say one more thing, and then the conversation turned out to last much longer, and ended with a kiss.

Valentine's Day was syrupy. It was trite enough that their more romantically inclined friends groaned, but it did not seem at all trite or syrupy to them. As Peter's last name was Patrick, he called Mary's father and prayed that St. Patrick's Day would be a momentous day for both of them.

Peter and Mary took a slow run to a nearby village, and had dinner at an Irish pub. Amidst the din, they had some hearty laughs. The waitress asked Mary, "Is there anything else that would make this night memorable?" Then Mary saw Peter on his knee, opening a jewelry box with a ring: "I love you, Mary. Will you marry me?"

Mary cried for a good five minutes before she could answer. And when she had answered, they sat in silence, a silence that overpowered the din. Then Mary wiped her eyes and they went outside.

It was cool outside, and the moon was shining brightly. Peter pulled a camera from his pocket, and said, "Stay where you are. Let me back up a bit. And hold your hand up. You look even more beautiful with that ring on your finger."

Peter's camera flashed as he took a picture, just as a drunk driver slammed into Mary. The sedan spun into a storefront, and Mary flew up into the air, landed, and broke a beer bottle with her face.

People began to come out, and in a few minutes the police and paramedics arrived. Peter somehow managed to answer the police officers' questions and to begin kicking himself for being too stunned to act.

When Peter left his room the next day, he looked for Prof. Johnson. Prof. Johnson asked, "May I give you a hug?" and then sat there, simply being with Peter in his pain. When Peter left,

Prof. Johnson said, "I'm not just here for academics. I'm here for you." Peter went to chapel and his classes, feeling a burning rage that almost nothing could pierce. He kept going to the hospital, and watching Mary with casts on both legs and one arm, and many tiny stitches on her face, fluttering on the borders of consciousness. One time Prof. Johnson came to visit, and he said, "I can't finish my classes." Prof. Johnson looked at him and said, "The college will give you a full refund." Peter said, "Do you know of any way I can stay here to be with Mary?" Prof. Johnson said, "You can stay with me. And I believe a position with UPS would let you get some income, doing something physical. The position is open for you." Prof. Johnson didn't mention the calls he'd made, and Peter didn't think about them. He simply said, "Thank you."

A few days later, Mary began to be weakly conscious. Peter finally asked a nurse, "Why are there so many stitches on her face? Was she cut even more badly than--"

The nurse said, "There are a lot of stitches very close together because the emergency room had a cosmetic surgeon on duty. There will still be a permanent mark on her face, but some of the wound will heal without a scar."

Mary moved the left half of her mouth in half a smile. Peter said, "That was a kind of cute smile. How come she can smile like that?"

The nurse said, "One of the pieces of broken glass cut a nerve. It is unlikely she'll ever be able to move part of her face again."

Peter looked and touched Mary's hand. "I still think it's really quite cute."

Mary looked at him, and then passed out.

Peter spent a long couple of days training and attending to practical details. Then he came back to Mary.

Mary looked at Peter, and said, "It's a Monday. Don't you have classes now?"

Peter said, "No."

Mary said, "Why not?"

Peter said, "I want to be here with you."

Mary said, "I talked with one of the nurses, and she said that you dropped out of school so you could be with me.

"Is that true?" she said.

Peter said, "I hadn't really thought about it that way."

Mary closed her eyes, and when Peter started to leave because he decided she wanted to be left alone, she said, "Stop. Come here."

Peter came to her bedside and knelt.

Mary said, "Take this ring off my finger."

Peter said, "Is it hurting you?"

Mary said, "No, and it is the greatest treasure I own. Take it off and take it back."

Peter looked at her, bewildered. "Do you not want to marry me?"

Mary said, "This may sting me less because I don't remember our engagement. I don't remember anything that happened near that time; I have only the stories others, even the nurses, tell me about a man who loves me very much."

Peter said, "But don't you love me?"

Mary forced back tears. "Yes, I love you, yes, I love you. And I know that you love me. You are young and strong, and have the love to make a happy marriage. You'll make some woman a very good husband. I thought that woman would be me.

"But I can see what you will not. You said I was beautiful, and I was. Do you know what my prognosis is? I will probably be able to stand. At least for short periods of time. If I'm fortunate, I may walk. With a walker. I will never be able to run again--Peter, I am nobody, and I have no future. Absolutely nobody. You are young and strong. Go and find a woman who is worth your love."

Mary and Peter both cried for a long time. Then Peter walked out, and paused in the doorway, crying. He felt torn inside, and then went in to say a couple of things to Mary. He said, "I believe in miracles."

Then Mary cried, and Peter said something else I'm not going to repeat. Mary said something. Then another conversation began.

The conversation ended with Mary saying, "You're stupid, Peter. You're really, really stupid. I love you. I don't deserve such love. You're making a mistake. I love you." Then Peter went to kiss Mary, and as he bent down, he bent his mouth to meet the lips that he still saw as "really quite cute."

The stress did not stop. The physical therapists, after time, wondered that Mary had so much fight in her. But it stressed her, and Peter did his job without liking it. Mary and Peter quarreled and made up and quarreled and made up. Peter prayed for a miracle when they made up and sometimes when they quarreled. Were this not enough stress, there was an agonizingly long trial--and knowing that the drunk driver was behind bars didn't make things better. But Mary very slowly learned to walk again. After six months, if Peter helped her, she could walk 100 yards before the pain became too great to continue.

Peter hadn't been noticing that the stress diminished, but he did become aware of something he couldn't put his finger on. After a night of struggling, he got up, went to church, and was floored by the Bible reading of, "You have heard that it was said, 'Love your neighbor and hate your enemy.' But I tell you, love your enemies and pray for those who persecute you." and the idea that when you do or do not visit someone in prison, you are visiting or refusing to visit Christ. Peter absently went home, tried to think about other things, made several phone calls, and then forced himself to drive to one and only one prison.

He stopped in the parking lot, almost threw up, and then steeled himself to go inside. He found a man, Jacob, and... Jacob didn't know who Peter was, but he recognized him as looking familiar. It was an awkward meeting. Then he recognized him as the man whose now wife he had crippled. When Peter left, he vomited and felt like a failure. He talked about it with Mary...

That was the beginning of a friendship. Peter chose to love the man in prison, even if there was no pleasure in it. And that created something deeper than pleasure, something Peter couldn't explain.

As Peter and Mary were planning the wedding, Mary said, "I want to enter with Peter next to me, no matter what the tradition says. It will be a miracle if I have the strength to stand for the whole wedding, and if I have to lean on someone I want it to be Peter. And I don't want to sit on a chair; I would rather spend my wedding night wracked by pain than go through my wedding supported by something lifeless!"

When the rehearsal came, Mary stood, and the others winced at the pain in her face. And she stood, and walked, for the entire rehearsal without touching Peter once. Then she said, "I can do it. I can go through the wedding on my own strength," and collapsed in pain.

At the wedding, she stood next to Peter, walking, her face so radiant with joy that some of the guests did not guess she was in exquisite pain. They walked next to each other, not touching, and Mary slowed down and stopped in the center of the church. Peter looked at her, wondering what Mary was doing.

Then Mary's arm shot around Peter's neck, and Peter stood startled for a moment before he placed his arm around her, squeezed her tightly, and they walked together to the altar.

On the honeymoon, Mary told Peter, "You are the only person I need." This was the greatest bliss either of them had known, and the honeymoon's glow shined and shined.

Peter and Mary agreed to move somewhere less expensive to settle down, and were too absorbed in their wedded bliss and each other to remember promises they had made earlier, promises to seek a church community for support and friends. And Peter continued working at an unglamorous job, and Mary continued fighting to walk and considered the housework she was capable of doing a badge of honor, and neither of them noticed that the words, "I love you" were spoken ever so slightly less frequently, nor did they the venom and ice creeping into their words.

One night they exploded. What they fought about was not important. What was important was that Peter left, burning with rage. He drove, and drove, until he reached Wheaton, and at daybreak knocked on Prof. Johnson's door. There was anger in his voice when he asked, "Are you still my friend?"

Prof. Johnson got him something to eat and stayed with him when he fumed with rage, and said, "I don't care if I'm supposed to be with her, I can't go back!" Then Prof. Johnson said, "Will you make an agreement with me? I promise you I won't ever tell you to go back to her, or accept her, or accept what she does, or apologize to her, or forgive her, or in any way be reconciled. But I need you to trust me that I love you and will help you decide what is best to do."

Peter said, "Yes."

Prof. Johnson said, "Then stay with me. You need some rest. Take the day to rest. There's food in the fridge, and I have books and a nice back yard. There's iced tea in the--excuse me, there's Coke and 7 Up in the boxes next to the fridge. When I can come back, we can talk."

Peter relaxed, and he felt better. He told Prof. Johnson. Prof. Johnson said, "That's excellent. What I'd like you to do next is go in to work, with a lawyer I know. You can tell him what's going on, and he'll lead you to a courtroom to observe."

Peter went away to court the next day, and when he came back he was ashen. He said nothing to Prof. Johnson.

Then, after the next day, he came back looking even more disturbed. "The first day, the lawyer, George, took me into divorce court. I thought I saw the worst that divorce court could get. Until I came back today. It was the same--this sickening scene where two people had become the most bitter enemies. I hope it doesn't come to this. This was atrocious. It was vile. It was more than vile. It was--"

Prof. Johnson sent him back for a third day. This time Peter said nothing besides, "I think I've been making a mistake."

After the fourth day, Peter said, "Help me! I've been making the biggest mistake of my *life*!"

After a full week had passed, Peter said, "*Please*, I *beg* you, don't send me back there."

Prof. Johnson sent Peter back to watch a divorce court for one more miserable, excruciating day. Then he said, "Now you can do whatever you want. What do you want to do?"

The conflict between Peter and Mary ended the next day.

Peter went home, begging Mary for forgiveness, and no sooner than he had begun his apology, a thousand things were reflected in Mary's face and she begged his forgiveness. Then they talked, and debated whether to go back to Wheaton, or stay where they were. Finally Mary said, "I really want to go back to Wheaton."

Peter began to shyly approach old friends. He later misquoted: "I came crawling with a thimble in the desparate hope that they'd give a few tiny drops of friendship and love. Had I known how they would respond, I would have come running with a bucket!"

Peter and Mary lived together for many years; they had many children and were supported by many friends.

The years passed and Peter and Mary grew into a blissfully happy marriage. Mary came to have increasing health problems as a result of the accident, and those around them were amazed at how their love had transformed the suffering the accident created in both of their lives. At least those who knew them best saw the transformation. There were many others who could only see their happiness as a mirage.

As the years passed, Jacob grew to be a good friend. And when Peter began to be concerned that his wife might be... Jacob had also grown wealthy, very wealthy, and assembled a top-flight legal team (without taking a dime of Peter's money--over Peter's protests, of course), to prevent what the doctors would normally do in such a case, given recent shifts in the medical system.

And then Mary's health grew worse, much worse, and her suffering grew worse with it, and pain medications seemed to be having less and less effect. Those who didn't know Mary were astonished that someone in so much pain could enjoy life so much, nor the hours they spent gazing into each other's eyes, holding hands, when Mary's pain seemed to vanish. A second medical opinion, and a third, and a fourth, confirmed that Mary had little chance of recovery even to her more recent state. And whatever measures been taken, whatever testimony Peter and Mary could give about the joy of their lives, the court's decision still came:

The court wishes to briefly review the facts of the case. Subject is suffering increasingly severe effects from an injury that curtailed her life greatly as a young person. from which she has never recovered, and is causing increasingly complications now that she will never again have youth's ability to heal. No fewer than four medical opinions admitted as expert testimony substantially agree that subject is in extraordinary and excruciating pain; that said excruciating pain is increasing; that said excruciating pain is increasingly unresponsive to medication; that subject has fully lost autonomy and is dependent on her husband; that this dependence is profound, without choice, and causes her husband to be dependent without choice on others and exercise little autonomy; and the prognosis is only of progressively worse deterioration and increase in pain, with no question of recovery.

The court finds it entirely understandable that the subject, who has gone through such trauma, and is suffering increasingly severe complications, would be in a state of some denial. Although a number of positions could be taken, the court also finds it understandable that a husband would try to maintain a hold on what cannot exist, and needlessly prolong his wife's suffering. It is not, however, the court's position to judge whether this is selfish...

For all the impressive-sounding arguments that have been mounted, the court cannot accord a traumatized patient or her ostensibly well-meaning husband a privelege that the court itself does not claim. The court does not find that it has an interest in allowing this woman to continue in her severe and worsening state of suffering.

Peter was at her side, holding her hand and looking into his wife's eyes, The hospital doctor had come. Then Peter said, "I love you," and Mary said, "I love you," and they kissed.

Mary's kiss was still burning on Peter's lips when two

nurses hooked Mary up to an IV and injected her with 5000 milligrams of sodium thiopental, then a saline flush followed by 100 milligrams of pancurium bromide, then a saline flush and 20 milligrams of potassium chloride.

A year later to the day, Peter died of a broken heart.

Hymn to the Creator of Heaven and Earth

With what words
shall I hymn the Lord of Heaven and Earth,
the Creator of all things visible and invisible?
Shall I indeed meditate
on the beauty of his Creation?

As I pray to Thee, Lord,
what words shall I use,
and how shall I render Thee praise?

Shall I thank thee for the living tapestry,
oak and maple and ivy and grass,
that I see before me
as I go to return to Thee at Church?

Shall I thank Thee for Zappy,
and for her long life--
eighteen years old and still catching mice?
Shall I thank thee for her tiger stripes,
the color of pepper?
Shall I thank thee for her kindness,

and the warmth of her purr?

Shall I thank Thee for a starry sapphire orb
hung with a million million diamonds, where
"The heavens declare the glory of God;
and the firmament proclaims the work of his hands.
Day to day utters speech,
and night to night proclaims knowledge.
There are no speeches or words,
in which their voices are not heard.
Their voice is gone out into all the earth,
and their words to the end of the earth.
In the sun he has set his tabernacle;
and he comes forth as a bridegroom out of his chamber: he will
exult as a giant to run his course."?

Shall I thank Thee for the river of time,
now flowing quickly,
now flowing slowly,
now narrow,
now deep,
now flowing straight and clear,
now swirling in eddies that dance?

Shall I thank Thee for the hymns and songs,
the chant at Church, when we praise Thee in the head of Creation,
the vanguard of Creation that has come from Thee in Thy
splendor and to Thee returns in reverence?

Shall I thank thee for the Chalice:
an image,
an icon,
a shadow of,
a participation in,
a re-embodiment of,
the Holy Grail?

Shall I forget how the Holy Grail itself
is but the shadow,
the impact,
the golden surface reflecting the light,
secondary reflection to the primeval light,
the wrapping paper that disintegrates next to the Gift it holds:
that which is
mystically and really
the body and the blood of Christ:
the family of saints
for me to be united to,
and the divine Life?

Shall I meditate
on how I am fed
by the divine generosity
and the divine gift
of the divine energies?

Shall I thank Thee for a stew I am making,
or for a body nourished by food?

Shall I indeed muse that there is
nothing else I could be nourished by,
for spaghetti and bread and beer
are from a whole cosmos
illuminated by the divine light,
a candle next to the sun,
a beeswax candle,
where the sun's energy filters through plants
and the work of bees
and the work of men
to deliver light and energy from the sun,
and as candle to sun,
so too is the bread of earth
to the Bread that came from Heaven,

the work of plants and men,
the firstfruits of Earth
returned to Heaven,
that they may become
the firstfruits of Heaven
returned to earth?

Shall I muse on the royal "we,"
where the kings and queens
said not of themselves"I", but "we"
while Christians are called to say "we"
and learn that the "I" is to be transformed,
made luminous,
scintillating,
when we move beyond "Me, me, me,"
to learn to say, "we"?

And the royal priesthood is one in which we are called to be
a royal priesthood,
a chosen people,
more than conquerors,
a Church of God's eclecticism,
made divine,
a family of little Christs,
sons to God and brothers to Christ,
the ornament of the visible Creation,
of rocks and trees and stars and seas,
and the spiritual Creation as well:
seraphim, cherubim, thrones
dominions, principalities, authorities,
powers, archangels, angels,
rank on rank of angels,
singing before the presence of God,
and without whom no one can plumb the depths
of the world that can be seen and touched.

For to which of the angels did God say,
"You make my Creation complete," or
"My whole Creation, visible and invisible,
is encapsulated in you,
summed up in your human race?"

To which of the angels
did the divine Word say,
"I am become what you are
that you may become what I am?"

To which of the angels did the Light say,
"Thou art my Son; today I have adopted Thee,"
and then turn to say,
"You are my sons; today I have adopted you;
because I AM WHO I AM,
you are who you are."?

So I am called to learn to say, "we",
and when we learn to say we,
that "we" means,
a royal priesthood,
a chosen people,
more than conquerors,
a Church of God's eclecticism,
a family of little Christs,
made divine,
the ornament of Creation, visible and invisible,
called to lead the whole Creation
loved into being by God,
to be in love
that to God they may return.

And when we worship thus,
it cannot be only us, for
apples and alligators,

boulders and bears,
creeks and crystals,
dolphins and dragonflies,
eggplants and emeralds,
fog and furballs,
galaxies and grapes,
horses and habaneros,
ice and icicles,
jacinth and jade,
kangaroos and knots,
lightning and light,
meadows and mist,
nebulas and neutrons,
oaks and octupi,
porcupines and petunias,
quails and quarks,
rocks and rivers,
skies and seas,
toads and trees,
ukeleles and umber umbrellas,
wine and weirs,
xylophones and X-rays,
yuccas and yaks,
zebras and zebrawood,
are all called to join us before Thy throne
in the Divine Liturgy:

> Praise ye the Lord.
> Praise ye the Lord from the heavens:
> praise him in the heights.
> Praise ye him, all his angels:
> praise ye him, all his hosts.
> Praise ye him, sun and moon:
> praise him, all ye stars of light.
> Praise him, ye heavens of heavens,
> and ye waters that be above the heavens.

Let them praise the name of the Lord:
for he commanded, and they were created.
He hath also stablished them for ever and ever:
he hath made a decree which shall not pass.
Praise the Lord from the earth, ye dragons, and all deeps:
Fire, and hail; snow, and vapours;
stormy wind fulfilling his word:
Mountains, and all hills;
fruitful trees, and all cedars:
Beasts, and all cattle;
creeping things, and flying fowl:
Kings of the earth, and all people;
princes, and all judges of the earth:
Both young men, and maidens;
old men, and children:
Let them praise the name of the Lord:
for his name alone is excellent;
his glory is above the earth and heaven.
He also exalteth the horn of his people,
the praise of all his saints;
even of the children of Israel,
a people near unto him.
Praise ye the Lord.

How can we know Christ
as the bridge between God and mankind
if we forget Christ
as the bridge between God
and his whole Creation?
Can a wedge come between the two?
Shall we understand the human mind
without needing to know of the body?
Shall we worship in liturgy at Church
without letting it create a life of worship?
Shall we say, "Let them eat cake?"

of those who lack bread?
No more can we understand Christ
as saving "Me, me, me!"
but not the whole cosmos,
of which we are head, yes,
but of which he is the greatest Head.

On what day do we proclaim:

> As the prophets beheld,
> as the Apostles have taught,
> as the Church has received,
> as the teachers have dogmatized,
> as the Universe has agreed,
> as Grace has shown forth,
> as Truth has revealed,
> as falsehood has been dissolved,
> as Wisdom has presented,
> as Christ awarded...
> thus we declare,
> thus we assert,
> thus we preach
> Christ our true God,
> and honor as Saints
> in words,
> in writings,
> in thoughts,
> in sacrifices,
> in churches,
> in Holy Icons;
> on the one hand
> worshipping and reverencing
> Christ as God and Lord,
> and on the other hand
> honoring as true servants
> of the same Lord of all

and accordingly offering them
veneration... *[Then louder!]*
This is the Faith of the Apostles,
this is the Faith of the Fathers,
this is the Faith of the Orthodox,
this is the Faith which has established the Universe.

Is it not the day
when we celebrate the restored icons,
because Christ became not only a human spirit,
but became man,
entering the Creation,
the Word become matter,
taking on himself all that that entails.

And all that that entails
means that Christ became matter
and that matter is to be
glorified in his triumph,
the same Christ
whose physical body was transfigured
and shone with the light of Heaven itself
and this was not an opposite
of what is to be normal
but rather transformed what is normal
so that our embodiment is to be our glory.
And this Christ,
who lived as a particular man,
in a particular place,
honored every time and place,
as the Nobel Prize for physics
honors not simply one chosen physicist per year,
but in its spirit
honors the whole enterprise of physics.
When Christ entered a here and now,
he honored every here and now,

and the Sunday of the restoration of icons
is not "The Sunday of Icons"
but
"The Sunday of Orthodoxy."
Christ was not a "generic" man
with no real time or place.
Christ entered a here and now
and his saints entered a here and now
and if he became what we are,
that we might become what he is,
the divine become human
that the human might become divine,
then if we are not to divide the Christ,
or truncate the Christ,
then his victory extends
to spirit shining through matter
in icons.
How can we praise Thee for this, O Lord?

Is not it all born up
in the scandal of the particular,
and we remember the woman in whom Heaven and Earth met,
who cannot be separated from the Church,
nor from the Cosmos,
to whom we sing
with the beauty of Creation?

Shall we recall his work in Creation
in the song to the woman
in whom Heaven and Earth met?

> I shall open my mouth,
> and the Spirit will inspire it,
> and I shall utter the words of my song
> to the Queen and Mother:
> I shall be seen radiantly keeping

feast and joyfully praising her wonders.

Most holy Theotokos, save us.

Beholding thee,
the living book of Christ,
sealed by the Spirit,
the great archangel exclaimed to thee,
O pure one:
Rejoice, vessel of joy,
through which the curse
of the first mother is annulled.

Most holy Theotokos, save us.

Rejoice, Virgin bride of God,
restoration of Adam and death of hell.
Rejoice, all-immaculate one,
palace of the King of all.
Rejoice, fiery throne of the Almighty.

Glory to the Father,
and to the Son,
and to the Holy Spirit.

Rejoice, O thou who alone
hast blossomed forth the unfading Rose.
Rejoice, for thou hast borne the fragrant Apple.
Rejoice, Maiden unwedded,
the pure fragrance of the only King,
and preservation of the world.

Both now and ever,
and unto the ages of ages.
Amen.

Rejoice, treasure-house of purity,
by which we have risen from our fall.
Rejoice, sweet-smelling lily
which perfumeth the faithful,
fragrant incense and most precious myrrh.

O Mother of God,
thou living and plentiful fount,
give strength to those
united in spiritual fellowship,
who sing hymns of praise to thee:
and in thy divine glory
vouchsafe unto them crowns of glory.

Most holy Theotokos, save us.

From thee, the untilled field,
hath grown the divine Ear of grain.
Rejoice, living table
that hath held the Bread of Life.
Rejoice, O Lady, never-failing
spring of the Living Water.

Most holy Theotokos, save us.

O Heifer that barest the unblemished Calf
for the faithful, rejoice,
Ewe that hast brought forth the lamb of God
Who taketh away the sins of all the world.
Rejoice, ardent mercy-seat.

Glory to the Father,
and to the Son,
and to the Holy Spirit.

Rejoice brightest dawn,

who alone barest Christ the Sun.
Rejoice, dwelling-place of Light,
who hast dispersed darkness
and utterly driven away
the gloomy demons.

Both now, and ever,
and unto the ages of ages. Amen.

Rejoice, only door through
which the Word alone hath passed.
By thy birthgiving, O Lady,
thou hast broken the bars and gates of hell.
Rejoice, Bride of God,
divine entry of the saved.

He who sitteth in glory
upon the throne of the Godhead,
Jesus the true God,
is come in a swift cloud
and with His sinless hands
he hath saved those who cry:
Glory to Thy power, O Christ.

Most holy Theotokos, save us.

With voices of song in faith
we cry aloud to thee,
who art worthy of all praise:
Rejoice, butter mountain,
mountain curdled by the Spirit.
Rejoice, candlestick and vessel of manna,
which sweeteneth the senses of all the pious.

Most holy Theotokos, save us.

Rejoice, mercy-seat of the world,
most pure Lady.
Rejoice, ladder raising all men
from the earth by grace.
Rejoice, bridge that in very truth
hast led from death to life
all those that hymn thee.

Most holy Theotokos, save us.

Rejoice, most pure one,
higher than the heavens,
who didst painlessly carry within thy womb
the Fountain of the earth.
Rejoice, sea-shell that with thy
blood didst dye a divine purple robe
for the King of Hosts.

Glory to the Father,
and to the Son,
and to the Holy Spirit.

Rejoice, Lady who in truth
didst give birth to the lawgiver,
Who freely washed clean
the iniquities of all.
O Maiden who hast not known wedlock,
unfathomable depth, unutterable height,
by whom we have been deified.

Both now, and ever,
and unto the ages of ages.
Amen.

Praising thee who hast woven
for the world a Crown

not made by hand of man,
we cry to thee:
Rejoice, O Virgin,
the guardian of all men,
fortress and stronghold and sacred refuge.

The whole world was amazed
at thy divine glory:
for thou, O Virgin
who hast not known wedlock,
hast held in thy womb
the God of all
and hast given birth
to an eternal Son,
who rewards with salvation
all who sing thy praises.

Most holy Theotokos, save us.

Rejoice, most immaculate one,
who gavest birth to the Way of life,
and who savedst the world
from the flood of sin.
Rejoice, Bride of God, tidings
fearful to tell and hear.
Rejoice, dwelling-place of the Master
of all creation.

Most holy Theotokos, save us.

Rejoice, most pure one,
the strength and fortress of men,
sanctuary of glory,
the death of hell,
all-radiant bridal chamber.
Rejoice, joy of angels.

Rejoice, helper of them
that pray to thee with faith.

Most holy Theotokos, save us.

Rejoice, O Lady,
fiery chariot of the Word,
living paradise,
having in thy midst
the Tree of Life,
the Lord of Life,
Whose sweetness vivifieth
all who partake of Him
with faith, though they
have been subject to corruption.

Glory to the Father,
and to the Son,
and to the Holy Spirit.

Strengthened by thy might,
we raise our cry
to thee with faith:
Rejoice, city of the King of all,
of which things glorious and worthy to be heard
were clearly spoken.
Rejoice, unhewn mountain,
unfathomed depth.

Both now, and ever,
and unto the ages of ages.
Amen.

Rejoice, most pure one,
spacious tabernacle of the Word,
shell which produced

the divine Pearl.
Rejoice, all-wondrous Theotokos,
who dost reconcile with God
all who ever call thee blessed.

As we celebrate this sacred
and solemn feast
of the Mother of God,
let us come, clapping our hands,
O people of the Lord,
and give glory to God who
was born of her.

Most holy Theotokos, save us.

O undefiled bridal chamber of the Word,
cause of deification for all,
rejoice, all honorable preaching
of the prophet;
rejoice, adornment of the apostles.

Most holy Theotokos, save us.

From thee hath come
the Dew that quenched
the flame of idolatry;
therefore, we cry to thee:
Rejoice, living fleece wet
with dew,
which Gideon saw of old,
O Virgin.

Glory to the Father,
and to the Son,
and to the Holy Spirit.

Behold, to thee, O Virgin,
we cry: Rejoice!
Be thou the port and a haven
for all that sail
upon the troubled waters of affliction,
amidst all the snares of the enemy.

Both now, and ever,
and unto the ages of ages.
Amen.

Thou cause of joy,
endue our thoughts with grace,
that we may cry to thee:
Rejoice, unconsumed bush,
cloud of light
that unceasingly overshadowest the faithful.

The holy children
bravely trampled upon the threatening fire,
refusing to worship created things
in place of the Creator,
and they sang in joy:
'Blessed art Thou and
praised above all,
O Lord God of our Fathers.

Most holy Theotokos, save us.

We sing of thee, saying aloud:
Rejoice, chariot of the noetic Sun;
true vine, that hast produced ripe grapes,
from which floweth a wine making glad
the souls of them that in faith glorify thee.

Most holy Theotokos, save us.

Rejoice, Bride of God,
who gavest birth
to the Healer of all;
mystical staff,
that didst blossom with the unfading Flower.
Rejoice, O Lady,
through whom we are filled
with joy and inherit life.

Most holy Theotokos, save us.

No tongue, however eloquent,
hath power to sing thy praises, O Lady;
for above the seraphim art thou exalted,
who gavest birth to Christ the King,
Whom do thou beseech
to deliver from all harm
those that venerate thee in faith.

Glory to the Father,
and to the Son,
and to the Holy Spirit.

The ends of the earth
praise thee and call thee blessed,
and they cry to thee
with love:
Rejoice, pure scroll,
upon which the Word was written
by the finger of the Father.
Do thou beseech Him
to inscribe thy servants
in the book of life, O Theotokos.

Both now, and ever,
and unto the ages of ages.

Amen.

We thy servants pray to thee
and bend the knees of our hearts:
Incline thine ear, O pure one;
save thy servants who are always sinking,
and preserve thy city
from every enemy captivity, O Theotokos.

The Offspring of the Theotokos
saved the holy children in the furnace.
He who was then prefigured
hath since been born on earth,
and he gathers all the creation to sing:
O all ye works of the Lord,
praise ye the Lord and exalt Him
above all for ever.

Most holy Theotokos, save us.

Within thy womb
thou hast received the Word;
thou hast carried Him who carrieth all;
O pure one, thou hast fed with milk
Him Who by His beck feedeth the whole world.
To Him we sing:
Sing to the Lord,
all ye His works,
and supremely exalt
Him unto the ages.

Most holy Theotokos, save us.

Moses perceived in the burning bush
the great mystery of thy childbearing,
while the youths clearly prefigured it

as they stood in the midst of the fire
and were not burnt,
O Virgin pure and inviolate.
Therefore do we hymn thee
and supremely exalt thee unto the ages.

Most holy Theotokos, save us.

We who once through falsehood
were stripped naked,
have by thy childbearing been clothed
in the robe of incorruption;
and we who once sat in the darkness of sin
have seen the light, O Maiden,
dwelling-place of Light.
Therefore do we hymn thee
and supremely exalt thee unto the ages.

Glory to the Father,
and to the Son,
and to the Holy Spirit.

Through thee the dead are brought to life,
for thou hast borne the Hypostatic Life.
They who once were mute
are now made to speak well;
lepers are cleansed,
diseases are driven out,
the hosts of the spirits of the air are conquered,
O Virgin, the salvation of men.

Both now, and ever,
and unto the ages of ages.
Amen.

Thou didst bear the salvation of the world,

O pure one, and through thee we
were lifted from earth to heaven.
Rejoice, all-blessed, protection and strength,
rampart and fortress of those who sing:
O all ye works of the Lord,
praise ye the Lord
and supremely exalt Him unto the ages.

Let every mortal born on earth,
radiant with light,
in spirit leap for joy;
and let the host of the angelic powers
celebrate and honor the holy feast
of the Mother of God, and let them cry:
Rejoice! Pure and blessed Ever-Virgin,
who gavest birth to God.

Most holy Theotokos, save us.

Let us, the faithful, call to thee:
Rejoice! Through thee, O Maiden, we have
become partakers of everlasting joy.
Save us from temptations, from barbarian
captivity, and from every other injury
that befalleth sinful men
because of the multitude of their transgressions.

Most holy Theotokos, save us.

Thou hast appeared as our
enlightenment and confirmation;
wherefore, we cry to thee:
Rejoice, never-setting star
that bringest into the world
the great Sun. Rejoice, pure Virgin
that didst open the closed Eden.

Rejoice, pillar of fire,
leading mankind to a higher life.

Most holy Theotokos, save us.

Let us stand with reverence
in the house of our God,
and let us cry aloud:
Rejoice, Mistress of the world.
Rejoice, Mary, Lady of us all.
Rejoice, thou who alone art immaculate
and fair among women.
Rejoice, vessel that receivedst
the inexhaustible myrrh poured out on thee.

Glory to the Father,
and to the Son,
and to the Holy Spirit.

Thou dove that hast borne the Merciful One,
rejoice, ever-virgin!
Rejoice, glory of all the saints.
Rejoice, crown of martyrs.
Rejoice, divine adornment
of all the righteous
and salvation of us the faithful.

Both now, and ever,
and unto the ages of ages.
Amen.

Spare Thine inheritance, O God,
and pass over all our sins now,
for as intercessor in Thy sight,
O Christ, Thou hast her that on earth
gave birth to Thee without seed,

when in Thy great mercy
Thou didst will to take the form of man.

To Thee, the Champion Leader,
we Thy servants dedicate
a feast of victory and of thanksgiving
as ones rescued out of sufferings,
O Theotokos:
but as Thou art one with might which is invincible,
from all dangers that can be
do Thou deliver us,
that we may cry to Thee:
Rejoice, Thou Bride Unwedded!

To her is sung:

More honorable than the cherubim,
and more glorious beyond compare than the seraphim,
thou baredst God the Word.
True Mother of God,
we magnify thee.

Shall we praise thee
for the beauty of a woman
with a child in her arms,
or a child nestled in her womb?

Mary is the one whose womb
contained the uncontainable God.

When that happened,
she gave him his humanity,
and there was an exchange of gifts.

Once you understand this exchange,
it changes everything.

She gave him
his humanity.
He gave her
grace,
the divine life,
as none before her
and none after.

The cherubim and seraphim are the highest ranks of angels.
'Seraph' means fiery one
and they stand most immediately in God's presence.

What is this fire?
Is it literal heat from a real fire?
Or is it something deeper,
something more fire-like than fire itself?
Would not someone who understood the seraphim
as the highest angels,
angels that burn,
would instead ask if our "real" fires
are truly real?
Is it emotion?
Or is it not "emotion"
as we understand the term,
as "deep love"
is not "hypocritical politeness"
as we understand the term?
Or yet still more alien?

Is there anything in our visible Creation
that can explain this?

If a man were to be exposed to this fire,
and he were not destroyed that instant,
he would throw himself into burning glass
to cool himself.

And yet an instant
of direct touch with God the Father,
were that even possible,
would incinerate the seraphim.

Then how can we approach God?

The bridge between Heaven and Earth:
the Word by which the Father is known,
the perfect visible image of the invisible God,
who has become part of his Creation.

When we look at the Christ, the Bridge,
and see the perfect image of God,
God looks at Christ, the Bridge,
and sees the perfect image
of mankind
and not merely mankind,
but inseparably the whole Creation.

How shall we worship the Father,
fire beyond fire beyond fire?

How shall we worship God,
holy, holy, holy?

It is a mystery.
It is impossible.
And yet it happens
in one who was
absolutely God and absolutely man,
and one who is
absolutely God and absolutely man,
bringing Heaven down to Earth,
sharing our humanity
that we might share in his divinity,

and bring Heaven down to Earth, that Earth may be brought up to Heaven.

There is a mystic likeness
between
Mary, the Mother of God,
the Church,
and the world,
feminine beauty
created, headed, and served
by a masculine revealed God
whom no one can measure.
His light is incomparably more glorious;
we can know the energies from God
but never know God's essence,
and yet to ask that question is
the wrong way of looking at it.
It is like asking,
"Which would you choose:
Compassion for your neighbor or common decency,
Being a good communicator or using language well,
Living simply or not wasting electricity?"

Christ and the Church are one,
a single organism,
and in that organism,
the rule is one unified organism,
not two enemies fighting for the upper hand.
I am one of the faithful,
and the clergy are not clergy at my expense.
We are one organism.
The Gift of the Eucharist does not happen,
except that it be celebrated by a priest,
and except that the people say, "Amen!"
The Church in its fullness is present
where at least one bishop or priest is found,

and at least one faithful--
and without the faithful,
the clergy are not fully the Church.
The "official" priest is priest,
not instead of a priestly call among the faithful,
but precisely as the crystallization of a priesthood in which
there is no male nor female,
red nor yellow nor black nor white,
rich nor poor, but Christ is all,
and is in all, with no first or second class faithful.
Every Orthodox,
every Christian,
every person
is called to be
part of a single united organism,
a royal priesthood,
a chosen people,
more than conquerors,
a Church of God's eclecticism,
made divine
a family of little Christs,
sons to God and brothers to Christ,
the ornament of Creation, visible and invisible,
called to lead the whole Creation
loved into being by God,
to be in love
that to God they may return.

So what can we do,
save to give thanks
for rocks and trees,
stars and seas,
pencils and pine trees,
man and beast,
faces and embraces,
solitude and community,

symphonies and sandcastles,
language and listening,
ivy vines and ivy league,
cultures and clues,
incense and inspiration,
song and chant,
the beauty of nature
and the nature of beauty,
the good, the true, and the beautiful,
healing of soul and body,
the spiritual struggle,
repentance from sin
and the freedom it brings,
and a path to walk, a Way,
one that we will never exhaust--
what can we do
but bow down in worship?

Glory be
to the Father,
and the Son,
and the Holy Spirit,
both now and ever,
and to the ages of ages.
Amen.

Meat

I was sitting at a table with my classmates, and there was one part of the conversation in particular that stuck in my mind. One of my classmates was a vegan, and my professor, who was Orthodox but usually was not as strict as some people are observing Orthodox fasts, said that he was challenged by that position. He talked about Orthodox monasticism, which usually avoids meat, and its implication that meat is not necessary. I wanted to contribute to that discussion, but my sense was that that wasn't quite the time to speak. When I explored it after that meal, it seemed more and more to be something that was part of a deep web, connected to other things.

What is Theophany? And what does it have to do with meat?

When I became Orthodox, one of the biggest pieces of advice the priest who received me (my spiritual father) gave me was to take five or ten years to connect with the liturgical rhythm. Now in the Orthodox Church advice from spiritual fathers is like a doctor's prescription in that what is given to one person may not be good at all for another: like a prescription given by a doctor, it is given to one person for that specific person's needs, and should not normally be seen as universal advice that should be good for everyone. However, that doesn't mean that advice is perversely designed to be useless to everyone else. I believe this was good pastoral advice not because of something ultimately idiosyncratic about me--something true of me but no one else--but because of something I share with a lot of other people, especially other Westerners.

In the Orthodox Church, there are days, weeks, and years as in the West, but what they mean is different. In some respects the similarity is deceptive. The biggest difference is less a matter of linear vs. cyclical time, as that in the West time is like money: people will say, "Time is money," and if it is a metaphor, it is none the less a metaphor that captures people's outlook very well. Time is like a scarce commodity; it's something you use to get things done, and you can not have enough, and run out of time. Language of "saving time" like one would save resources is because the way people treat time is very close to how one would treat a commercial resource that you use to get things done. This may be deeply rooted in some Orthodox, especially Western members of the Orthodox, but instead of time being like a limited supply of money, time is like a kaleidoscope turning. There are different colors--different basic qualities held in place by worship, prayer at home, fasting from certain foods, feasting, commemorating different saints and Biblical events, and being mindful of different liturgical seasons--and they combine in cycles of day, week, and year, given different shades as people grow. Again, this is much less like "Time is money." than "Time is the flow of colors in a kaleidoscope."

One of those seasons is called "Theophany," and it is defined by the third most important feast in the year. I am writing in that season, and it seems an appropriate enough season to write this piece. It fits Theophany.

"Theophany" means "the manifestation of God." That word does not refer to icons or animals. But the way that God was manifest in Theophany has every relevance to icons and animals.

Theophany is the celebration of the Lord Jesus' baptism in the river Jordan, and at one point this was not celebrated from what we now celebrate in Christmas. At that baptism, the Father spoke from Heaven and said, "This is my beloved Son, in whom I am well pleased," the Son was baptized, and the Spirit appeared in the form of a dove. The Trinity was made manifest, but more to the point, the Trinity of God was made manifest *to and through material Creation.*

The Fathers have never drawn a very sharp line between Christ the Savior of men and Christ the Savior of the whole creation. This isn't something the Fathers added to the Bible: the Son of God has entered into his creation so completely that the Bible itself says that Christ is "the image of the invisible God, the firstborn of every creature: For by him were all things created, that are in heaven, and that are in earth, visible and invisible, whether they be thrones, or dominions, or principalities, or powers: all things were created by him, and for him: And he is before all things, and by him all things consist."

When Christ was baptized in water, he blessed the whole creation. Yes, he set a precedent for his followers. I wouldn't want to diminish that. But if you draw the line and say the story is relevant to our being baptized but nothing more, you have cut off its fundamental relevance to the whole Creation. The Orthodox liturgy never forgets the rest of the created order, and the liturgy for Theophany crystallizes this in the service for the blessing of the water:

> Great art thou, O Lord, and wonderful are thy works, and no word doeth justice to the praise of thy wonders; for by thy will thou didst bring out all things from nonexistence into existence; and by thy might thou dost control creation, and by thy providence thou dost govern the world. Thou it is who didst organize creation from the four elements, and crowned the cycle of the year with four seasons. Before thee tremble supersensual powers; thee the sun praiseth, the moon worshippeth, the stars submit to thee, the light obeyeth, the tempests tremble, the springs worship thee. Thou didst spread out the heaven like a tent; thou didst establish the earth on the waters. Thou didst surround the sea with sand. Thou didst

> pour out the air for breathing. Thee do the angelic hosts serve; thee the ranks of the archangels do worship, the many-eyed cherubim, the six-winged seraphim, as they stand in thy presence and fly about thee, hiding with fear from thine unapproachable glory...

And shortly the water is blessed, opening a season of blessing in which people's houses are blessed, icons are blessed, people are blessed, and so on. To be human is to be created for worship, but it is not only humans; every material creature and every spiritual creature (the "supersensual powers", the "many-eyed cherubim", and other figures in the liturgy quoted above) are not only created to worship but have a place in what could be called a united organism.

People today are seeking a harmony between man and nature, and some people may wonder if Orthodoxy has a basis for such a harmony. The answer is a yes and no. Let me explain.

If we ask a different question, "What would harmony between humans and technology be? What would a society look like?" then there might be an image of people caring for machines, adapting themselves to them, and so on and so forth. And that image, or that projection, would lead to a deceptive image among societies today. If we are talking about the kind of technology in the first world today, then the first world today not only is better attuned with technology than the second or third world, but has done something with technology that is simply without parallel in the first 99.999% (literally) of the time humans have been around. Although some other nations like Japan may have a slight edge over my native USA, I'm going to focus on the USA for the simple reason that I know it better.

In the USA, which has something about technology that exceeds what has been done in the same vein in the first 99.999% of the time humans have been around, there are people who develop technology and are carefully attuned to it. And the culture is optimized to support technology in a way that I didn't appreciate until I lived in the second world. You may be able to count on your fingers the number of societies that have ever managed, in the entire history and prehistory of the human race, to be more attuned to technology. And yet the society is not what one would imagine if one tried to imagine a society in harmony with technology.

This is a society with a minority current making Luddite arguments about why computers are bad (and to me the arguments have more weight than some might suspect). There are also people who have no academic axe to grind about the sociological effects of video games, but hate learning new programs. The predominant computer operating system is the most insecure operating system, the one that most exposes its users to viruses and worms--better operating systems are available, at very least from a security and privacy perspective, *for free* in some cases, but the industry standard is the one that leaves its users most vulnerable to malicious software. Furthermore, people do not hold technology as objects of reverence, or at least most people don't. Not only is it not a big deal to dispose of no-longer-wanted technology, but "planned obsolescence" means that technology is made to be thrown away. When technology is broken, it will probably be replaced instead of being repaired. You can be very educated and know very little about technology. And the list goes on.

Now I ask: Is this attunement with technology? And the answer is "Yes," but it is the kind of attunement seen in real society (perhaps more perfectly in Japan and other places), not what one would imagine as "harmony with technology." The difference between the two is like the difference between romantic relationships--the kind you have with another flesh-and-blood human who has things that your imagination didn't put there--and romantic fantasies. In fact people don't think in terms of "harmony with technology;" to ask if American culture lives in harmony with technology is a question few Americans would ask.

Does Orthodoxy have a key to harmony with nature? Let me give one clue. No single technology--not SUVs, not environmentally incorrect inks, not styrofoam--dictates a heavy environmental footprint. Even if there were no soy inks, the printer in itself need not dictate environmental damage. What dictates environmental damage is waste. And Orthodoxy never tells a society what technologies it may and may not use--when someone ran an anti-SUV advertisement asking, "What would Jesus drive?" Orthodoxy may well agree with the archaeologist who in essence said, "Speaking as someone who's done excavations in the Holy Land's rugged terrain, you basically need an SUV, and Jesus with his twelve disciples would have driven a Hummer." (This does not mean that we all need Hummers. I get rides from people but don't own a car myself.) Even if Orthodoxy does not give a list of what technologies its people can't use, Orthodoxy does join voices with many other Christians in saying that part of the walk of virtue is living simply, meaning using what you need but being willing to ask "Do we need what we can afford?" instead of just "Can we afford what we need?" This simplicity is not lived consistently in the first world, but the classical virtue of living simply, formulated at a time when people simply were not thinking in environmentalist terms, has implications for appropriate stewardship of the earth. Living simply has usually been conceived as something that deals with rich and poor--almost all people in the first world who have a home would be considered rich--but it is part of a right ordering that will rightly orient people and society to the material world.

But there is another side to the issue. In the Western way of looking at it, there is a fundamental opposition between harmony (shaded by equality) and domination (shaded by inequality). Harmony, by definition, does not include domination. But the way the Eastern Church approaches it fits neither into the Western boundaries of harmony nor the Western boundaries of domination. The link between man and nature needs harmony, but it is incomplete if it cannot include domination and even destruction. The PETA position, admittedly extreme for people who have animal rights sympathies, is that a duck is a rat is a goat is a boy. To them, meat is murder, not just as a way of exaggerating something deep, but in a literal sense. And I cannot agree with that. If I could kill a goat and save a girl, I would do so. And beyond that, I eat meat, more than most people (at least before low-carb diets came in vogue, and perhaps after).

When I was a boy, my art teacher told the class to get smocks, and my father gave me an unwanted shirt--but he would have given me his best shirt if I needed it. I used it and it kept me from getting clay and paint on my other clothing. (In other words, I destroyed it.) That wasn't the only thing of my parents' that I destroyed. I destroyed the meals my mother cooked for me (usually by eating them and throwing away as little as possible--you wouldn't want them when I was done). I destroyed things that weren't working by taking them apart to see what was inside. I destroyed clothing that my mother brought for me, usually by wearing it out. If my parents had back every penny they spent on something that I destroyed, they would have a good deal more money.

However, my parents did not raise me to be a destructive man. The smock is an example of justified destruction. The fact that my father gave me one of his shirts to destroy as a smock does not mean that it didn't matter if I destroyed his shirts. He would have been quite bothered if I had rubbed red clay onto all of his shirts. Quite a lot of the destruction I did was appropriate. It was justified destruction within a context, and I believe it illustrates what it means to say both that destruction can be permissible, and that destruction matters. To speak of justified destruction is both to say that destruction can be justified and that justification *needs* to be justified: it is acceptable to destroy a dress shirt when a smock is needed, but destroying a dress shirt *needs* to be justified, and is not appropriate when it is not justified.

The concept of "raw materials" applied to the natural world isn't a very Orthodox concept, for much the same reason that it would seem strange to interpret our house as merely a bunch of raw materials for me to destroy at will. The examples above notwithstanding, my parents did not want me to be destructive, and the fact that I was permitted to destroy things was not the central truth of the matter. It would be much closer to the truth to say that I was in that home to grow into a Christian and a man, and be a member of that family. There was also a footnote that said I could destroy some things in some circumstances. But even the things which I was permitted to destroy were not "raw material". A shirt has value in itself, as a shirt, even if it is used as a smock.

The problem with considering the items in my parents' house is raw material is that *they have both status and value* independently of what I might get out of destroying them. It might matter that I would benefit from destroying the shirt by using it as a smock, but the heart of the matter is that "potential for making a smock" is neither the only status nor the only value of a dress shirt.

An icon, a picture painted to help make spiritual realities manifest, has value as the emblem of a view of the Creation where science and materialism do not tell the whole story, where matter has spiritual qualities above the legitimate observation of scientists, and where saying "Nature is simply what science describes" is as fundamentally erroneous as saying "Your value as a human being is simply what you get when you subtract your financial liabilities from your assets." If an icon is spiritual, if it is part of God manifesting himself through matter and restoring matter to his circle of blessing, then there is something inadequate if the only meaning to "matter" is "what science describes." Matter is a part of the treasurehouse of God, and the icon is spiritual not as an exception to inert matter and raw material, but as the crystallization of something at the heart of Creation. Seeing the natural world as raw material is almost as strange from an Orthodox perspective as seeing people in terms of their financial net worth. It's the same kind of error.

Of the possessions in my parents' house, not are equal, and it makes a difference whether I am destroying a plastic cup or a landscape painted by my mother. In God's own house with his treasures, not all are of equal value. There are some of these treasures that exist, in their way reflecting a God who is existence itself: rocks, for instance. There are some possessions which exist in a deeper sense, having an existence that is alive, a reflection of a God who is not only Being itself but Life itself. Then, beyond these oaks and roses, there are treasures which exist and even live in a way that moves: gazelles and badgers. As the pinnacle of material creation and the microcosm that brings together the material and the spiritual, are creatures that exist, live, and move in out of rationality--on a richer and more interesting understanding of "rationality" than most people would associate with the word today. That would be the realm of men. Lastly, there are bodiless rational spirits. rank on rank of angels.

We can destroy treasures that exist, live, and even move, and some people think that in dire circumstances we may destroy the highest of material treasures, the ones that are rational. But that does not mean that it's all the same to destroy rocks, plants, and animals. Destroying a plant--to make a vegan's meal, for instance--is more serious than smashing a pebble. (Unfortunately, you can't live off of a diet of rocks.) Destroying an animal is far more serious, and there are sources which suggest it is more a concession than what we would think of today as a right. You can find people arguing that meat is more of a condition to weakness and medical concerns than something healthy people should need to resort to.

In Judaism, "kosher" is not only a matter of whether the meat comes from a clean animal like a cow or a sheep or an unclean animal like a pig. It also is a matter of how the animal was slaughtered.

The butcher says a blessing over the animal and then makes a single motion with a knife that has to be sharp, and is specified so that the animal dies as swiftly and painlessly as possible. Its lifeblood is also to be poured out as thoroughly as possible--because the animal's life belongs to God, not to us, and even if we may kill it, Judaism at least frames acceptable slaughter in a way that shows respect for the animal killed.

If we look at a Jewish shepherd with his flock of sheep, under second temple Judaism, and a contemporary (to him) pagan

Greek swineherd with his flock of pigs, they (or at least the Jew) would have seen themselves as complete opposites, at least after taking into account that they both raise a group of animals. There may have been a difference in whether all the animals were being raised for meat, but let's ignore that for the sake of argument. The Greek swineherd might have found the comparison rather insulting: to Greeks, Jews were these antisocial people who wouldn't mingle in polite company and for some reason treated one of the most delicious meats (pork) as if it were something revolting and putrid. In other words, Greeks perceived Jews as rather a bit weird, a beer or two short of a six-pack. The Jew, however, would have *certainly* found the comparison insulting to the extreme: not only was this figure a goy, a heathen dog, but he was raising pigs. Saying that he was like a *swine*herd is offensive in much the same way it would be offensive to tell a UPS delivery driver who is proud of helping the business world and contributing a little to help the economy run smoothly, that that she is like a gang's drug runner because they both deliver packages, whether the packages are productive business documents or street drugs. The Jew would have been more offended by the comparison, but for people who raise flocks of animals, the Jew and Greek would have seen themselves as very different.

But let's compare them to how pigs are raised today, in today's factory farming. Pigs spend almost their entire lives in tiny cells, with an hour of artificial light a day--the rest of the day being surrounded by darkness--constricted in cells too small for them to turn around, deprived of a herd animal's normal contact with other animals from its herd, traumatized not only by sounds but by the unending stench of rotting feces. The workers who treat them come down with atrocious respiratory diseases--and they are exposed to the vile air for a few hours a day instead of 24/7 as the pigs are. I don't believe that feeding animals antibiotics is innately wrong, but with pigs it serves as an inappropriate band-aid for the damage caused by a dungeon--if that is a strong enough word--which is such a toxic environment that feeding the animals constant antibiotics actually makes a marked difference in the number of pigs killed by the life in their dungeon.

If we compare the Jew and the Greek herd-keepers, suddenly they look the same, and some things take on a new significance. Both allowed their herds to graze at least some of the time. Both allowed their animals to have natural contact with other like animals as part of a herd. Both raised their animals in daylight. Both raise their animals in places that gave them not just room to turn around, but room to move about normally. And now I'd like to ask what the Jewish shepherd (at least) would have thought of the factory farming way of raising (in the example above) pigs. Or, if you prefer, a rabbi.

Do you know how when you step on a tack or stub your toe, you feel tremendous pain, *immediately*, but if you get in a car accident and really need to go to the emergency room, it takes a while for the pain to register? My suspicion is that kosher slaughter techniques leave an animal unconscious and possibly dead before the pain has had time to register. Even if it is not painless slaughter, the specific rules are motivated by a principle that reduces suffering in a timespan of only a few minutes. And non-kosher slaughter, unless people go out of their way to cause suffering, cannot come anywhere near the suffering which factory farming inflicts on pigs. For that matter, it's not clear how one would go about creating a torment-filled slaughter technique that would come anywhere near the lifelong suffering animals experience in factory farming. My suspicion is that people who are criminally convicted of cruelty to animals (at least in the U.S.) cause nowhere near the suffering before the animal is dead that factory farms do. To the best of my knowledge, Orthodox Judaism has not made rules about how an animal must be treated for its entire life to provide kosher meat, but if the rules were being articulated today, I suspect that the rules would recognize that lifelong torment is more of a problem than failing to kill an animal quickly and with a minimum of pain (as well as pouring its blood out as a reverent recognition that the life of an animal belongs to the Lord).

Before further discussion about factory farming's evil side, I would like to explain what it has allowed. Raising animals the traditional way is expensive, requiring a lot of land and a lot of manpower. Factory farming--stacking animal cells in warehouse-like fashion and in general treating animals like mere machines--is a way to automate and mechanize the production of both meat and animal products like eggs and cheese. It is a tremendous way to cut corners, and the result is that things that come from animals are drastically reduced in price, drastically cheaper.

It is difficult, at least in the first world, for people to understand that for most of history people have not been vegetarians but neither did they eat meat every day. There have been a few hunter tribes that had a meat-based diet. For most people whose food came from farms, bread or rice has been the staple food. Meat was for special occasions or a seasoning; eating meat every day would seem strange to most people, like ordering lobster every time you feel like a snack, or drinking Champagne with every meal. Meat, being an expensive thing to produce, was something people didn't have as the basis for normal meals. If you are an American adult--and you have not made a conscious choice early in your life to drastically reduce or eliminate meat from your diet--then you have almost certainly eaten much more meat than Jesus did. This does not automatically mean that we shouldn't eat meat ever, or that we should eat meat rarely, but it does suggest that eating meat every day is not really the traditional way of doing things, even if most people were not vegetarians. A lot of people today love lobster and Champagne, but that doesn't mean it's normal in my society to have them every day. It might be telling that the "Our Father" Jesus gave doesn't say, "Give us today our daily meat," but "Give us today our daily bread." That doesn't mean that we shouldn't eat meat, but it seems not to assume, as people sometimes do, that meat is the main food.

I'd like to point out something more about American culture. Where I was growing up, I heard that a restaurant,

Dragon West, had been closed down for improper use of domestic animals. For those of you who don't have X-ray goggles, "improper use of domestic animals" is an opaque bureaucratic euphemism for the fact that they were serving dogs as food. The reason the restaurant was shut down has to do with the fact that eating dogs is culturally offensive to much of American culture, and there is a reason for that.

There's a rule in America that if you keep a particular type of animal as a pet, you don't eat that kind of animal's meat. The rule is not absolute, and part of it is that most kinds of pets (carnivorous cats, for instance) would make poor livestock, and most kinds of livestock (behemothic bovines, for instance) would be hard to keep in a suburban home. And the rule isn't absolute. Aside from rabbits, people swallow goldfish, although they seem to do that precisely *because* it crosses a line. But once you acknowledge a jagged border, it's not just true that we happen not to eat the most common pets; many Americans would find the idea of eating a dog or cat to be nauseating. And it's deeply seated enough to close down a restaurant.

You can, at some restaurants I've been to, order fish head curry. That doesn't get a place shut down, but it breaks another rule. More specifically, it breaks the rule that meat shouldn't give obvious clues that it came from an animal. Fish, which look the least like people, can be sold with their heads on. But unless you go out of your way, chickens are sold without head and feathers, and red meat and pork (which are from non-human mammals) is sold with even fewer clues that it's some of the flesh of a slaughtered animal. Not that a detective couldn't figure it out, but meat is sold in a form that hides where it came from, and people buying or eating beef would probably be grossed out by having a cow's severed head nearby. Surely some of this is for economic reasons, but Americans who eat meat tend not to want to be reminded where it came from.

Lastly, people can be disturbed by the idea of eating certain kinds of "gross" things, things that creep and crawl--eating a tarantula or scorpion would be disturbing. (Interestingly, this rule seems to have a clause that says, "except if it came from the sea," so the tarantula's watery cousin the crab is fair game, as is the scorpion's cousin the lobster.) That observation aside, the animals used to evoke horror in movies are generally not used as food.

My point in this is not to say that we all have rules, or think that only Orthodox Jews and Muslims have dietary rules. Even if the last rule has a strange exception, these rules are not random.

A devout Muslim will not eat pork and a devout Hindu will not eat beef, but the reasons are opposite: to the Muslim, a pig is an abomination, while to the Hindu, the god Shiva's steed is a cow, and it would be an affront to Shiva to kill his steed for food. So we have abstinence out of disrespect and our of respect.

In the last rule I gave, "Thou shalt not eat anything creepy," is an abstinence out of disrespect: spiders and lizards are dirty things that aren't clean enough to eat. But neither of the first two rules is like this. The rules against eating animals that could be used as pets, and meat that looks too much like it came from an animal, are not rules of disrespect but rules of "Don't remind me that an animal was killed for this." The average suburbanite would rather be fed by meat from a kind of animal he has never interacted with closely--i.e. a cow--than think, "This came from a dog like the one I had growing up."

This adds some complexity to the picture of "America is a place where people eat lots of meat and that's that." It suggests that, even if we eat lots of meat, there is something residual, a reticence that tries not to know that meat comes from slaughtered animals. (That is even without adding any knowledge of what it means for livestock to be raised under factory farming, which in my mind far outweighs the slaughter itself.)

Not all meat is created equal.

I had a bear of a time learning what specific conditions animals are raised under. Animal rights activists tend to want to treat animals as people, and only tell about what is inhumane, never what is humane, and so they will never tell you that beef cattle are raised under much nicer conditions than pigs. The people involved in factory farming seem not to advertise what they are doing. This makes not the easiest conditions to find out how much cruelty is associated with different things. (Or maybe I was just looking in the wrong places.)

What I was able to find--or the impression I was able to get--makes for a sort of ascending scale of cruelty, moving from least cruel (no more cruel than traditional animal husbandry) to most cruel. This scale isn't perfect, but it's the one I use.

Before we get on the scale, there is soy milk (which I've found to be available at grocery stores, and the chocolate is easiest to get used to), soy cream cheese, and so on. I still haven't gotten the hang of liking tofu. I've found some other soy substitutes not to taste equivalent, but to taste good enough, and soy is claimed to have a complete protein signature.

At the base of the scale, the purest and most humane end, include ocean caught fish and seafood, and organic and free range anything. Organic food (which goes a little further than free range food--free range means that livestock can move about, *free range*, instead of being confined to coffinlike cells) can be found if you look for it at some supermarkets, and can be found at yuppie, granola music listening places like Whole Foods, which stacks exclusively organic produce, is pure as the driven snow, and has prompted a nickname of Whole Paycheck.

Next up the list are beef and mutton. Beef cattle do end up in fattening lots where they have little space, but they spend most of their lives growing up on open grazing land, able to move about, see sunlight, and be part of a herd.

Next up are eggs and dairy products. Because of the moral tenor of factory farming, animals can be treated cruelly even if they're not exactly being raised for their meat, and *if you order a cheeseburger, there's more cruelty in the cheese than in the burger.* Dairy cattle live much like pigs, although less of their lives (and therefore less cruelty) goes into producing a gallon of milk than a comparable amount of pork.

Last on the list are chicken, pork, turkey, and (the worst) veal. Many people know veal is cruel; pork and chicken are not much better. Chickens have a space roughly equal to a letter-sized paper folded in half, and farmers melt much of their beaks off (this is called "debeaking" by the farmers and the literature) because the living conditions cause so much fighting that the chickens would kill each other if they had their beaks and could peck like normal chickens would.

That is one of two things the animal rights crowd won't tell you. There's one other major thing I found that they don't advertise.

In the Orthodox tradition, part of the story is fasting, which doesn't mean abstaining from all foods and drinking only water, but usually means abstaining from some foods. The requirement on paper is to essentially go to a vegan diet (shellfish are allowed; oil and alcohol aren't) and avoid most meat and animal products. This is more of a measuring stick than a requirement on paper, and some Orthodox bishops are concerned that new converts do not fast strictly. But, among people that observe fasting, most people go at least a notch or two closer than usual to a vegan diet. A little less than half the year has some fast or other, and the fast can be relaxed to some degree while still being observed. There are seasons of fasting, as well as days of the week.

What I realized in relation to fasting is that I hadn't expected what fasting would really do. Giving up some of my favorite tastes was obvious, and I experienced that. But craving meat and not giving into that craving came up, and I don't know that I consciously expected that, but it didn't surprise me. What did surprise me was consciousness, or more properly the effect it had on my consciousness.

Fasting quiets sinful habits and makes it easier to fight them. But at the same time, it drains energy and puts your mind in a fog. I have reason to believe that's not the final effect, that your body responds differently over time, but fasting affects different people somewhat differently, and the effect on me is quite strong.

What I realized, that animal rights activists will not tell you, was that the main difference in giving up meat (temporarily or permanently) is not the taste; it's not even really the craving, even if you fight a strong craving. It's consciousness, and when one friend said he was going to cut meat mostly out of his diet as he married his mostly vegetarian fiancée, I strongly urged him to monitor his state of consciousness.

When I eat more than a little Splenda, it makes me sick--nothing life-threatening or anything like that; I don't need a medical alert bracelet. But Splenda doesn't agree with me. If I eat a little, nothing happens. If I eat a bit more than that, I feel mildly sick. If I eat a lot, not only will I feel sick but nature will call with a louder-than-usual voice.

It's a shame, really. Every other artificial sweetener I've tried doesn't taste right; it tastes like something that's meant to taste like sugar, but fails. Splenda tastes like sugar's cousin come in for substitute duty, instead of complete strangers dressed up to vaguely resemble sugar. And I'm not the only person who likes the taste.

Actually, I don't think it's a shame at all. Perhaps it has its downsides: I suddenly can't eat most desserts, because at least where I buy desserts it's hard to find a dessert sweetened with real, honest sugar. If you can't eat Splenda, you can't eat most desserts. And perhaps I will have to turn down more than a tiny serving of some hand-cooked desert made by the friend I am visiting. But there's something to real, honest sugar, and it betrays something about Splenda.

A couple of friends in Kenya sent a newsletter trying to explain to the Western mind that people value a ring of oil as evidence of a stew's richness, that bread lists its calories as how much energy it provides for hard work, and they underscored that the calorie is a unit of energy. This is a totally different attitude from in the U.S., when calories count as strikes against food.

It is also a healthier attitude, which underscores that food is eaten to nourish the body. Now God, in his generosity, has made it a pleasure as well, but we don't need the pleasure, and we do need the nutrition (i.e. nourishment).

Splenda represents an effort to sever the link between eating and nourishment. It may be physically healthier to eat one ice cream bar sweetened with Splenda than with sugar, but it is not spiritually healthier, and there may be hidden consequences to the message, "I can eat and eat and not get fat." Not only is that bad for the spirit, in that it causes you to fall short of the full stature of being human. If you think about it, it may end up being bad for the waistline.

Splenda is, in short, a very attractive invitation to become a moral eunuch.

In contrast to this, I remember a plaque with a picture of a pig, which said, "Eat to live. Don't live to eat." It is the same mindset as Richard Foster saying (I think quoting someone), "Hang the fashions. Buy only what you need." Maybe he was talking about clothes, but it applies to foods too.

I try to eat animal products and meat, as much as are necessary for me be able to function. Unfortunately, I've found that I need a lot to function, partly for medical reasons. When I am receiving hospitality, I eat freely from what is offered to me; when I buy food, I buy a lot of beef, tuna, and chocolate soy milk. I try to get the minimum I need to function, and to take as much as I can from the lowest end of the cruelty scale. (I try. Sometimes I eat more than I need.) I also try to avoid wasting food and *really* try to avoid wasting meat--if it bothers me to see a pig raised in cruelty so I can eat a pork chop, it would be even worse for that pork chop to be thrown into the trash.

But there's something wrong with that. I don't mean that I chose the wrong private response to this dilemma. I think that as far as private responses go, it's at least tolerable. Perhaps other people have chosen different responses, and maybe it could be better, but the problem is that it is a private response in the first place.

PETA, officially "People for the Ethical Treatment of Animals" and labelled by some as "People Eating Tasty Animals," tend to be the sort of people Rush Limbaugh would have lampooned when he wanted to give the impression that all liberals were crackpots. They made a gruesome TV commercial telling children to run from their fisherman fathers, apparently for much the same reason you'd run from a serial killer. They've probably done quite a lot that will prevent moderates and conservatives from taking animal welfare concerns seriously. But there is one area in which they are perfectly rational.

If, as they believe, meat is literally murder, and if, as they believe, imprisoning animals under lifelong conditions of misery is morally equivalent to imprisoning humans under lifelong conditions of misery, then it is entirely inappropriate to say "I'll privately choose to be a vegan and you can privately eat your meat, and we can disagree without being disagreeable." Whatever else they may have wrong, what they have right is that society's default placement for the matter, of private decisions where people exercise their own private judgment on what if any dietary restrictions it may be. If they are completely wrong, and there is nothing wrong with veal, then maybe they have a private right to eat as if their erroneous beliefs are true, but if substantial parts of their claims are true, even the claims I have made, then there are real problems with the way American culture frames it.

I think I'm going to have to leave this approach "depracated without replacement"; I don't see anything better that could believably replace it.

I've been told I'm good with animals. I certainly love pets, other peoples' as well as my own: when I visit certain friends, I usually have a pet on my lap.

There was one point when a friend was moving into the area, and (for reasons I don't understand) asked me to stay with her dog, who was afraid of men. (Even though there were women in the group of friends who had come to help her.) At the beginning, it was very clear that the dog was nervous about being at the other end of a leash from me. But after half an hour, the dog's head was in my lap as I petted him, and when the group came, he was jumping up and down and wanted to meet the men as well as the women in the group. Part of what happened was because I knew how to approach slowly and let an animal get used to me, but part of it was probably something else.

That is probably the most exotic, or at least most impressive, story I can muster about my being good with animals.

If I visit friends with pets, I usually ask to see the pets. And I believe my family's warm atmosphere is part of why our cat is nineteen years old and still catches mice. This is *not* to say that we love our cat more than one friend, whose dog was hit by a car, or another friend, whose dog died of cancer. But it *is* to say that she might not have lived nearly so long if we merely gave her food and water, and that when she was attacked and was found curled up and not moving, she desparately needed a vet's attention, but I'm not sure she would have pulled through if she didn't have the love and prayers she received. (As it is, we are delighted that she pulled through and is back to being her old sweet self.)

When I left to study at Fordham, I moved to an apartment where pets were not allowed--not dogs, not goldfish. (And even if they were allowed, I wouldn't want to buy a pet that I wasn't reasonably confident I could care for properly with vacations, moves, etc. I wouldn't want to put a pet to sleep because it was no longer convenient to me.) So, I thought, I knew the perfect creative solution. I would buy a Furby--a furry stuffed animal that talks and moves, due to the technology inside. (In other words, a pet that wouldn't make messes or upset the powers that be.)

So I tried to convince myself that I could enjoy it as a pet, and for a while I thought I was successful: the Furby spoke its own language, and I learned a few words, being fond of languages. It would respond to my commands at least some of the time. The perfect pet for my situation... and it took a while before I acknowledged that there was something creepy about it. It wasn't creepy when it just stood there, looking like a stuffed animal and adding color to my room. But when it opened and closed its eyes, the technology seemed different from what I was expected. It almost seemed like the unnatural un-life of a vampire. I knew, of course, that it would run according to technology, and having done a master's thesis about artificial intelligence running into a brick wall, I knew that it wouldn't be truly intelligent. Yet I didn't count on the creep effect. Now the Furby stands as a decoration in my room, one I like looking at. But it isn't really to conserve battery power that I don't activate it very often. I recognize it as an impressive technical achievement, but not as a pet.

There's a spark of something that is there in a real animal that isn't there in a robot dressed in a stuffed animal costume, and it was driven home to me when I tried to pretend that it didn't make a difference. There is something special about existing, and there is something more special about living as a plant does, and something about the moving force that is an animal. Something that I can enjoy when I am with pets.

What is the point of this? Am I saying that being an animal lover is an obligation? No. I do not believe that the minimum acceptable requirement is being an animal lover. I don't think there is any moral imperative to learn how to deal with animals or have the faintest desire for a pet. But I would say that it is part of the spectrum of things that are acceptable. Not everyone needs to be a big animal lover, but it is an appropriate exercise of freedom. Not everyone needs to be a wine afficionado, but it makes sense to savor subtle differences in flavor and aroma for good wines that doesn't make sense with Mountain Dew. Slowly savoring a tiny taste of different years of Mouton Cadet rouge is not incongruous; slowly savoring a tiny taste of different years of Mountain Dew is absurd. It might me good for making a delightful lampoon of wine snobs, but Mountain Dew does not merit a treatment ordinarily reserved for wine. For the same reason, there is something that fits about luxuriating on a waterbed that does not fit about trying to luxuriate and savor a sleeping bag on a hard floor. There is no moral obligation to seek out a waterbed or even a bed, but there's a difference between a waterbed and a floor. Similar things could be said about painting with oil paints versus trying to paint with SAE 10W-40 motor oil. There's something there to animals that means that they make much better pets than shampoo bottles, so that being an animal lover is a fitting response whether or not it is a moral obligation. And that "something there" is present whether or not you are an animal lover.

There's something there. The "something there" of animals undergirds the possibility of people enjoying pets as some of us do, a "something there" that is not human and is less than humanity, but is something more than almost anything else in nature. There is also "something more" than machinery, and while there are not ethical problems about cruelty in how we treat machinery, there is a dimension to a farm animal that isn't there for economic assets in general. That means that there are ethical concerns surrounding meat and animal products even after some of us acknowledge that God has given us authority to slaughter his creatures.

Animal rights activists tend to think animal rights means treating animal rights as human. When people have treated me as human, they have given me a bedroom and made other rooms available. They have spent time with me, and made good food available--not raw unless there was good reason to serve it raw. They have given me Christmas presents and a million other signs of respect that animals do not merit. If I looked at things in terms of rights (I don't), I would draw a much narrower and much more modest list of rights for animals: being part of a herd, moving about out doors, seeing sunlight during the day, and so on. Nothing about beds and cooked foods, but treated like an animal, which is much less than being treated as human, but it's also different from being treated like a mere piece of machinery.

This leaves loose ends untied. I haven't explained why the breeding that went into the breed of 96% of turkeys sold in America (which causes an ungodly amount of meat to grow on a skeleton and beast that really aren't built to carry anywhere *near* that much weight--imagine the frame of a compact car supporting the bulk and weight of a full-fledged SUV) is cruel, and the breeding of housecats (which also introduces profound changes that some animal rights activists call out-and-out cruel) is appropriate stewardship with regard to God's creation. And this article is dense enough without exploring all of those. Environmentally conscious readers may not be pleased to note that my ranking of cruelty encourages people to buy foods that have some of the worst environmental footprint--a pound of beef is said to require 4000 gallons of our scarce water. You can make meat with less impact on the environment if you are willing to cut corners, not only economically but morally. But I would argue that cruelty concerns are heavier than even environmental. And those are presumably not the only loose ends I've left. But there are a couple of points I would like to underscore.

First, thinking in terms of "raw material" is inappropriate. Destruction may be justified, but if so it is justified destruction of items that have something to them besides what economic use we might be able to find. The whole system of factory farming treats animals as mere economic assets who cannot suffer or whose suffering is not as important as making the most money. That causes terrible, usually lifelong suffering. Cruelty to animals matters.

Second, cause as much cruelty as you need to, but not more. Try to have the lightest footprint that doesn't cause trouble to you--trouble meaning something more than "A cheese and bacon omelet would really hit the spot." (In my case trouble meant difficulty concentrating on my studies, and since then I've learned what my body can handle.) Eat to live. Don't live to eat. Remember that not all foods are created equal. Aside from soy, organic animal products and meat, and sea-caught fish and seafood are by far the least cruel; beef is more cruel than these, but *less* cruel than animal products like milk, cheese, and eggs; dairy and other animal products are less cruel than most meats, including turkey, pork, chicken, and especially veal. If you are eating meat because it tastes good and not because your body needs its nutrition and energy, that is unnecessary.

Third, caring about the living conditions of farm animals has been framed as a liberal thing. That may be because there's a problem which arose, and liberals have been better at waking up to something conservatives should have been noticing. If you are dubious of my credentials as a conservative, I invite you to read Our Food from God, published in a Christian journal that argues long and hard against even the more moderate forms of feminism.

It's not just liberals who have a strong moral ground to criticize factory farming. It's just that liberals have been quicker to wake up and say, "Houston, we have a problem."

Seeing animals only as financial assets whose suffering is not important, instead of God's treasures which may be judiciously destroyed but have value independent of their economic usefulness, is the same basic error as seeing a person in terms of financial worth. The error is more grievous in seeing a person in terms of money, but that same basic error--as opposed to keeping a light footprint and trying to keep to justified destruction--has caused terrible animal suffering. Consider ways in which you might limit suffering you cause, and consider emailing a friend a link to **http://JonathansCorner.com/writing/meat/**. And maybe visit the store locator for **Whole Paycheck, er, Whole Foods**.

The Watch

Metacult: So, Pater, I was thinking--wait a minute; I hear someone scratching at the door.

Janra: Hi, Vespucci. How are you?

Vespucci: Doing well. Take a seat.

Janra: Where?

Vespucci: Anywhere.

Janra: *Anywhere?*

Vespucci: Anywhere...

Off! *Off!* Get *off* my lap! Only my wife is allowed to sit there. You know that. Anyways, the *Radical Gadgets* catalogue came in today...

Janra: By the way, I phoned the company today. I think I can get some World War II vintage mechanical--

Vespucci: Don't even *think* about it. If you--

Pater: Easy, brothers. As you were saying?

Vespucci: As I was saying... *Radical Gadgets* has the most interesting tools. The cover product this month was an email filtering package that uses Bayesian filtering techniques to block unwanted messages.

Janra: *That's* original! I checked Freshmeat today, and I think they only have half a dozen well-known anti-spam packages, not counting lesser products and tools that have just been released. Does *Radical Gadgets* always find products this original?

Vespucci: But it is original. And it's not an anti-spam package. It has nothing to do with spam.

Pater: Huh?

Vespucci: Let me explain. You know that Bayesian filtering looks at a message and uses statistics to guess what category it belongs to, right?

Pater: Yes; go on.

Vespucci: But that will work whether you use it for incoming or outgoing e-mails. Most people use the filtering techniques on incoming e-mails, to try and reduce the fire hose of spam coming in. But you don't have to stop there. You can also filter outgoing e-mails.

Pater: Why would I want to filter the e-mails I send *out*?

Vespucci: You've never sent a flame? Come on; I remember a couple of times that you flamed me over something minor, and sent a very embarrassed apology when I waited two weeks and simply sent it back, and asked you to read it aloud, and tell me whether that's what you want me to hear from you. And it's not just you. When you're talking with a person face to face, there are two eyes looking at you and reminding you that a person hears every cutting word you say. That doesn't stop conflicts, but it does mitigate some of the abrasive things we're tempted to say. On a computer, it seems like there's just a keyboard and pixels--no person you can actually hurt. So people hit harder, and you have incredible flamewars, often between people who conduct themselves like responsible adults when they're talking to someone face to face. It's possible to learn discipline, of course, and conduct yourself maturely, but all too many people don't realise there's a discipline you have to learn even if you're mature.

And so instead of just assuming that the only bad e-mails are offensive messages from people who've never seen you, telling you that part of your body isn't big enough and you need to buy their snake oil, or that you're impotent, or that you're not man enough for a relationship with a real woman and will have to content yourself with pixels on a screen--apart from these, there are offensive messages that you send out and then wish you could somehow take back and delete.

And this program does just that. Once you've trained it on your sent mail folder, it watches messages you send out, and uses the same Bayesian technology that's so powerful in identifying spam, and identifies when you're writing something you'll regret later. Then it saves it, quarantining it in a separate folder until you come to your senses and delete it.

Pater: That's... um, I'm going to go to their computer and order it from their website. Please excuse me for a moment. I really need to--

Metacult: Sit down, Pater. You're not going to e-mail out any flames while we're here talking.

Vespucci: Hmm... um, I hadn't meant to have a big discussion about the anti-flame software. There were several things that caught my attention, but what caught my eye most was a watch that keeps exceptionally accurate time.

Pater: Huh? Who would need a more accurate way to keep time? Most cultures find an hour to be a short time, and a cheap digital watch keeps more accurate time than a $5000 Rolex, because our watches are too accurate already. It would be awfully hard to explain our to-the-second accuracy to an aboriginal--I can't see why, besides pride that wants a possession to boast about, someone would benefit from a more accurate watch.

Vespucci: Oh, but there is benefit--worth paying $5,000 for a digital watch. Even worth having to change the batteries too often.

Pater: How?

Vespucci: The watch doesn't just have an oscillating quartz crystal; it has an array of sensors in the watchband that measure skin temperature and conductivity, pulse, even a clever estimate of blood pressure, and feeds all of these into an embedded chip with some extraordinarily clever software.

This software takes these data and gets a picture of the person's emotional state. You know how time flies when you're having fun?

Pater: Didn't Einstein explain his theory of relativity by saying, "When a man sits with a pretty girl for an hour, it seems like a minute. But let him sit on a hot stove for a minute--and it's longer than any hour. That's relativity."

Vespucci: Um... that has nothing to do with the theory of relativity, and I'm not interested in discussing Einstein's spacetime now. If Einstein said that, he probably had a merry twinkle in his eye. But...

Come to think about it, that is a pretty good picture. The watch estimates your emotional state for one purpose: it keeps track of how long time seems to be passing. It has a normal timer that can count forty minutes until dinnertime, but it can also tell you how long the wait will *feel* like. And that's something no other watch can do.

Metacult: So it deals with subjective time? I read a book once which was trying to argue that time could be understood as something *besides* the number a machine has counted to. It talked about how a small child will ask Mom how long she's leaving for, and Mom's answer--she's really trying to avoid feeling guilty about leaving the child alone--are singularly unhelpful for a child trying to figure out how much perceived time must be endured before Mom returns.

Vespucci: Yes, and the minute-hour quote captures that. All watches tell what time it is from a machine's perspective. This is the only watch that tells time from a human perspective.

Metacult: Wonderful. What does it take into account besides clock ticks and the person's emotional state?

Vespucci: Huh? What else contributes to our experience of time besides the physical time and our psychological state?

Pater: Your question betrays nominalism. The way you've framed things shuts out the true answer.

Vespucci: We're entering the third millenium; I don't see why you're dragging in a controversy from medieval times.

Janra: Mmmph. Excuse me. I think I need a glass of water.

Metacult: Sit down, Janra. And don't look at me like that. I'm going let you answer that.

Janra: Certainly. Here are the steps to hunt a bear: First, fire your gun. Second, aim your gun. Third, locate a bear. Fourth, buy a gun.

Metacult: Try again.

Janra: Clothing to wear in winter: a heavy coat, then on top of that a good sweater or two, then two shirts and two pair of pants, then underwear, with woolen socks over your boots.

Metacult: Please be serious.

Janra: I *am* being serious.

Metacult: Then be mundane.

Janra: Oh. That's another matter entirely.

> Your entire approach is backwards and inside-out, as backwards as trying to shoot a bear before you have a gun, and as inside-out as wearing your anorak next to your skin.
>
> How? Let me respond to your second comment. If I said, in the most reverent of tones, "We're standing at the forty-second latitude and eighty-seventh longitude," you'd think I was making a mountain out of a molehill: yes, we're at a particular latitude and longitude, but what does that have to do with the price of eggs in China? It's true, but what does that have to do with anything we're discussing? Yet people say, "We're entering the third millenium" as if it is this great statement of far-reaching consequences, the sort of thing that should settle a matter. As you yourself did.
>
> People in the Middle Ages often did not know what year it was, or even what century, any more than people today know what latitude and longitude we're at--quick--do you know what latitude and longitude *you're* at? The reason is that we think the past is under a glass bell, where we humans are living our lives while those odd and quaint creatures under the bell are not the same as us. And it doesn't need to be that way. For a long time after Shakespeare's death, when people put on Shakespeare, they didn't try to reconstruct period accurate costumes. Why? Did they not know that Shakespeare lived long before them? Perhaps, but they also recognised that Shakespeare was a human who worked with human problems and wrote human drama, and that the reason his plays are worth performing is not because they're old but because they're timelessly *human*. And we forget this when we take great

care to dress actors in funny costumes that tell people that this is something quaint from long ago and far away.

You know that many of your physical possessions that make up the physical world come from far away: when you buy something at Target, and make no effort to find treasures from faroff land, you buy a lamp that was made in China or underpants that were made in Mexico. You know that the whole world is interconnected, so even if you don't go hunting off for exotic imports, a great many of the things you buy were made far away.

You can as much live without ideas from bygone ages as you can live in a house you built with your own hands--or for that matter, be born in a house you built with your own hands. That isn't how things work. Nominalism is one of innumerable ideas that has survived, just as the custom of using pots and pans has survived.

Vespucci: If it's one of innumerable ideas, why pay it that much attention?

Janra: Because I can count on my fingers the number of conceptual revolutions that are more important today than nominalism. Trying to understand how people think today without looking at nominalism is like trying to look at a summer meadow without seeing plants. There are other important ideas, but this one makes the short list.

Vespucci: Then why have I not heard more about nominalism, when I hear people talking about postmodernism, for instance, or modernism? And what is nominalism to begin with?

Janra: For the same reason a fish won't tell you about water. Modernism and postmodernism are both nominalism writ large; nominalism is a seed, whose flower is modernism, and whose fruit is postmodernism.

Vespucci: Hmm. I hear the distinct accent of a person laboring in the prison of one idea.

Janra: Bear with me. Nominalism may be seen as the lock on a prison: we need to pay close attention to the lock to see if there's any way to open it. Then, if we can get out, let us see if there are not many more ideas available after we have paid proper attention to nominalism.

Now what is nominalism? In a sentence, nominalism says, "There's nothing out there; it's all in your head." A nominalist doesn't literally mean "nothing" is outside our heads; you can't put on a watch and say, "I refute nominalism thus."

Vespucci: But it was a non sequitur when--

Janra: Yes, I know, I know. Another tangent. But let's forget about saying that matter is just in people's heads and not something external to mind. As I was saying, you can't put on a watch and say, "I refute nominalism thus." But if we really follow nominalist logic, you can't put on a watch. You can have nerve impulses that result in the motion of some elementary particles, but a watch is a tool-to-tell-time-which-you-wear-on-your-wrist, and a tool-to-tell-time-which-you-wear-on-your-wrist does not and cannot exist in nature. All the *meaning* that makes those atoms a watch can only exist in minds, and for the same reason what-we-call-a-watch can't have the time displayed on its face. It can have elementary particles that are placed like so and interact with light just so, but the meaning that can read a time in that configuration isn't at all in the atoms themselves; it's in your head. This is clarified in a distinction between "brute fact" and "social reality:" brute fact is what exists outside of minds and social reality can only exist in minds, and almost anything humans value consists of a small amount of brute fact and a large portion of social reality--larger than most people would guess. Everything is either brute fact or social reality.

Pater: Is the boundary between brute fact and social reality a brute fact or a social reality?

Metacult: Shut up.

Janra: Imagine three umpires at a baseball game: the first says, "I calls 'em as they are." The second says, "I calls 'em as I sees them." But the third says, "Some's strikes, and some's balls, but they ain't nothing 'til I calls 'em."

With apologies to Kronecker, God created cold matter. All else is the work of man.

Pater: Whoa. Is the basic faculty that lets man create social reality derived from brute fact or social reality?

Janra: Shut up.

Now I have been showing what happens when you push nominalism a good deal further than non-scholars are likely to do. But in fact nominalism has been seeping into our consciousness for centuries, so that we might not find the claim that nature is beautiful to be a mistake, but we see with nominalist eyes and hear with nominalist ears. Most of people across most of time have understood and experienced symbols very different from how a nominalist would.

If we assume that matter is basically something cold and dead, devoid of spiritual properties, then of course a symbol can only exist in the mind, a mental connection between two things that are not connected by nature. Any similarity is in the eye of the beholder, or if not that, is at least a coincidence that isn't grounded on anything deeper. There is no organic connection.

But if we look at how people have understood symbols, their understanding has to do with a view of reality where a great many things are real, where a symbol bespeaks a real and spiritual connection. The crowning jewel of this understanding of symbol was the claim that man is the image of God. When Christians talked about man being the image of God, they were not talking about what we would understand by a photograph or a painting, where pigments are arranged in such a way that an observer can tell they were meant to look like God; they meant a real and organic connection that went far beyond a mere representation of God; they meant that we were what you would think a kind of magical statue which not only represented God, but embodied his actual presence: God's presence operates in us in a real way, and every breath we breathe is the breath of God.

Now the reason we began discussing nominalism was that you said something, and I said, "That question betrays nominalism." Do you remember what you said?

Vespucci: No.

Janra: We were discussing what I consider to be a very interesting watch, and you asked what could contribute to our experience of time besides what an ordinary watch tells, and our emotional state.

That question betrays nominalism. You were in essence asking what could interest us in time besides the brute fact of what most watches tell, and the social, or at least mental, reality of our emotional state.

But there's a world of other things out there.

Vespucci: But what else is there?

Metacult: Hmm. I think we need to work a bit harder to help you look at what you believe. You've been keeping up on superstring theory, right?

Vespucci: Yes. I loved the explanations I could get of relativity, and I love how scientists can turn our commonsense notions upside down.

Metacult: Do you know any classical, Newtonian physics?

Vespucci: I did in high school. I've forgotten most of it now, but I don't remember it being nearly as exciting: a lot of math to go through to get at common sense.

Metacult: May I instead suggest that your common sense is a nonmathematical version of Newtonian physics?

Newton's physics was big on grids: everything was placed on a grid of absolute space, and absolute time. And it connected rooms the wrong way: different places are on the same meaningless grid, but they're not connected besides the grid.

To the medieval mind, it wasn't so. Each space was its own little world as far as Newton was concerned. But they were connected spiritually. There is an icon of two saints from different centuries talking, and the medieval mind was comfortable with this because it saw things other than "but they're from other parts of the spacetime grid!"

Vespucci: But what does this have to do with time? It seems to me you're going off on a tangent.

Metacult: Ok, back to time. Time isn't just a grid adorned by emotions. It's spiritually connected. You yourself are not self-contained.

Pater: And there's liturgical time. One of the things that shocked me was that people seem to have *no* time. It helped me to appreciate the colorful time I had breathed. I was stunned when people experienced time as torture. I experienced it as a sacrament, a channel of God's grace.

From other conversations, I get the impression that the liturgical year isn't real to you: one source of holidays among others. But it is real: interlocking cycles of day, week, year, so that you are breathing in this rhythm and are given something to live in each moment. Sometimes you're feasting; sometimes you're fasting; often you're given something to meditate on.

Vespucci: So the watch would do a more complete job if its little computer were programmed to keep track of the liturgical cycles? I think the engineers could do that.

Pater: Errmmmmm...

Metacult: I think what he means, but cannot articulate, is that what a computer could make of the liturgical cycles are *not* the place that makes liturgical time. They are more of a doorway into the place, into a room that the Spirit blows. If the watch were to keep track of that, it would have to have, not more sophisticated computer programming, but something else altogether, something sensitive to spiritual realities.

Pater: And that's just what a scientific computer, even a very small one, cannot do. Science works on nominalism. It's brought a lot of good stuff, but it can't perceive or work with spiritual qualities, any more than a pair of binoculars will improve your hearing. And that's fine when you recognise that spiritual qualities are left out, but the temptation is to say, "Because science is so powerful, it sees everything that's real." And a watch designed by scientific engineering can do scientific things, but if it were to try and see liturgical time from the inside, it would inevitably kill what breathes in it.

Janra: So if we were to imagine a watch that keeps track of time, true time, it would need not only sensors and a miniature computer, and a time-keeping quartz crystal, but something attuned to spiritual realities.

Pater: If that were possible. In my culture, we never wear watches. The best watch would be no watch, or perhaps a rock on a wristband, where if you go to it looking for trivia, it doesn't give what you're looking for--and in so doing, reminds you of something important, that you need to look elsewhere.

Janra: What about a watch that had a rock alongside the things we've just described?

Pater: Ermmm...

Janra: And what would men's and women's models look like? Would the rocks be respectively rough and smooth?

Metacult: Actually, men's and women's experience of time differs significantly, so if you had a watch with a truer way of telling time, there would be a much bigger difference than men's watches being heftier and women's watches being slender.

Janra: How?

Metacult: I remember one time when you were talking with a new mother, and whenever the baby needed care, you stopped talking so that Mom could pay attention to her new son. It was a thoughtful gesture, and one that wasn't needed.

Janra: Why not? I'd have wanted to be allowed to give the child my full attention.

Metacult: I know. So would most good men. A man's particular strength is to devote his full attention to a task. A woman's particular strength is to lightly balance several tasks, giving genuine attention to each. That mother was perfectly able to give attention to her son and listen to you at the same time. That's why she looked at you, slightly puzzled and with an attention that says, "I'm listening," when you stopped talking.

And there are other differences as well. If there is a situation that colors a man's understanding of time, it is a brief period of intense pressure. A woman's understanding of time more has the hue of a longer period that requires sustained attention. And even that misses something. The difference between a man's experience of time and a woman's is not so much like a difference between numbers as a difference between two colors, or sounds, or scents. It's a qualitative difference, and one that is not appreciated--usually people feel in their heart, "She's treating time the same way I do, but doing an unexplainably bad job of it."

Vespucci: I forgot to tell you, the watch also asks when you were born.

Pater: Why? To remind you if you forget your birthday?

Vespucci: I'm surprised, Pater. It's so it can keep track of your age. You experience time differently as you grow. What seems like an hour when you're five only seems like half an hour when you're ten, or fifteen minutes when you're twenty, or five minutes when you're sixty. Time seems to go faster and faster as you grow: there's one change between when you're a child and an adult, and senior citizens say that every fifteen minutes it's breakfast. The quality and pace of time change as you age, which is why young people think youth lasts forever and the rest of us think it vanishes. They say that once you're over the hill, you begin to pick up speed.

Pater: What does "over the hill" mean?

Vespucci: Um...

Metacult: He really doesn't understand. To him, aging is about maturing and growing, not only for children, but adults as well. He values his youth as a cherished memory, but he's enjoying his growth and looking forward eagerly to the joy awaiting him in Heaven. He doesn't understand your self-depracating humor that speaks as if aging were a weakness or a moral failing.

Vespucci: Ok.

Metacult: Which reminds me. One of the ways my experience of time has changed as I have grown has been to recognize that time flows faster and faster. For some people, this is a reason to try way too hard to be healthy--taking care of their bodies, not because their bodies should be taken care of, but to try and postpone the inevitable. But I'm looking forward to the Heaven that's getting closer and closer, and I am delighted by a glimpse into the perspective of a God who created time and to whom all times are both soon and now.

But the other major change is more internal, more a matter of discipline. I used to live in hurry, to always walk quickly and love to play video games quickly. Then I set foot in Malaysia, and something changed.

There was a difference, which I imperfectly characterized as life being lived more slowly in Malaysia. Which is true, or was for me, but is somewhat beside the point. And I experienced the joy of living more slowly. You know how I've thought that it takes humility to enjoy even pride, and chastity to enjoy even lust. At that point I would have added to those two that it takes slowness to enjoy even haste.

Vespucci: So you tried to be as slow as you had been quick?

Metacult: Yes. I observed that I had been obsessed with time under the tyranny of the clock, and so I tried to abolish time by being slow. Which isn't right; besides chronos, the time a clock can measure, there is kairos, relational or task-oriented or creating time, where you are absorbed in another person or a task, and there time is a glimmer of eternity. And I was interested in the idea of living time as the beginning of an eternal glory, which Pater understands much better than I ever will. First I tried to negate time and live as something less-than-temporal, and I am slowly realizing that instead it means embracing time and entering something more-than-temporal.

In liturgical time--and Pater could say much more about this than I--it flows. Here it moves quickly, there it moves slowly, and there it spins in eddies. It isn't just the speed that flows; it's the color, if you will. Just as the priest is the crowning jewel of the priesthood every person is called for, so the touch of Heaven as we worship is the crowning jewel of what time is meant to be.

And I had also been realizing that I had sought to escape time, and not cherish it as God's good creature. Most recently, I am trying to... There's a famous quote by Oliver Wendell Holmes, saying, "I wouldn't give a fig for the simplicity on this side of complexity, but I'd give my life for the simplicity on the other side of complexity." Now I'm looking for a time that is on the other side of complexity: not the mundane ordinariness of disfigured time, but a beautiful ordinariness on the other side of this complexity we've been discussing.

Vespucci: How do you think that will work?

Metacult: I don't know. Part of it has to do with the metaculture you used for my nickname. I don't simply breathe in my culture and ask "How else could it be?", but am in the odd position of being able to step into cultures but never be absolutely at home. And have part of me that doesn't fit. That's not quite right; I do connect, partly in a way that is basically human, and partly in a way that is--

Janra: Don't try to explain. That would take an hour.

Metacult: At any rate, a fair number of people talk about living counterculturally, and one way you can live counterculturally is let live time as a blessing rather than a curse. People who say technology determines our lives are almost right, and that *almost* makes a world of difference if you're willing to live counterculturally. The pressure on us to live in hurry is not a pressure that no one can escape. It is a pressure that few try to escape in the right way--but you can, if you try and go about it the right way.

But quite a lot of the rest of it has to do with very basic parts of the Christian life. God wants us to seek him first, and when we do, he knows full well what else we need. "Seek first the Kingdom of God, and all these things will be given to you as well." includes a life where time unfolds as a rainbow or a river, something of both color and flow, like the year with its beauty in due season.

Vespucci: Do you see time as a line or a circle? Something that keeps moving in a direction, or something that does the same thing over and over again?

Metacult: Both, of course. God is revealing himself in history and transforming it to his ends. And there is decay; decay follows a line down. In our lives, we are progressing towards Heaven or Hell, and in each day... here we meet the cycles, but if we live well, the cycles in our lives aren't just an aimless meandering, but like a man who keeps running through a ditch, digging. In one way, he's going to the same places again and again, but in another way, he's going deeper--and he may meet both the earth's warmth in winter (or coolness in summer), and the water of life. The line moves through circles.

Janra: So what would make the perfect watch?

Vespucci: Are there any we haven't covered?

Metacult: Umm... we've looked at one big change from a normal watch--instead of adding a calculator, that *Radical Gadgets* catalogue had a watch that tries to tell a more human time by taking your age and emotional state into account as well as what most watches tell. That was sort of a Pandora's box. I think we could all agree that that watch was leagues more human than any normal watch... and it was just human enough to reveal how un-human watches are.

Vespucci: How?

Metacult: When the only kind of watch kept track of seconds, it was easy enough to think that time was simply what a watch told. But when one watch started to pay attention to how you feel...

It was kind of like when you've been in the freezing outdoors for a long time, so long that it still hurts a little, but you can almost ignore it. Then you come inside, and THEN it stings. It's not until you enter a genuinely warm room that you realize how cold and numb you really are.

The watch in that catalogue was just human enough to reveal how un-human watches, and the time that they tell, are. It did what no other watch could. It's enough of a success to be a *spectacular* failure. Someone brought up liturgical time, which led to the suggestion that the watch be programmed to keep track of liturgical time. And then we stumbled into a hole with no bottom. Why can't a computer keep track of liturgical time? Well, you see, the Spirit does more than just follow calculations... A watch would need far more than better electronics to do that, far more than scientific engineering can provide. Although I did like the suggestion of adding a rock. Even if I don't see how to make a rock sensitive to women's time and men's time. Or rather, what to do to appropriately respect the difference.

Vespucci: Janra, what you said about nominalism interests me. Could you give a more complete explanation?

Janra: I'd love to, but I need to be somewhere next month.

Vespucci: Please be serious.

Janra: I *am* being serious.

Vespucci: Then be mundane.

Metacult: He *is* being mundane. If you'd like a good introduction, read Philip Sherrard's *The Rape of Man and Nature: An Enquiry Into the Origins & Consequences of Modern Science*. In it, Sherrard says almost nothing about time and everything about the things time is connected to. I think it goes overboard, but if you read it and pay attention to the haunting beauty that keeps coming up, then you'll learn something about being human--and living in human time. It doesn't use the word 'nominalism' very much, but it says quite a lot about it.

Vespucci: Are there any other things you've all left out?

Metacult: Only about two billion. I've talked about kairos as an absorbed time instead of a time when you're watching the clock. What I haven't talked about as kairos as a divinely appointed time, where you are in a divinely orchestrated dance, and you are free, and yet your movements are part of the divine plan. We are human, not by "just" being human, but by allowing the divine to operate in us; it is the divine, not the human, that we need most to be human. I haven't discussed that. We haven't discussed, in connection with nominalism, how there is a spiritual place in us where we meet God, and we have the ability to reason from what we see, and in tandem with nominalism we have become impoverished when both functions are dumped on the reasoning ability and we don't know where we can meet God, where our minds connect with the very Reason that is God himself. It makes a difference whether we experience time through both our reasoning ability and this spiritual meeting-place, or through our reasoning ability alone.

I also haven't talked about turning back the clock. When people rightly or wrongly believe there is a golden age they've lost, and try to re-create it, they end up severing connections with the recent past and even the golden age.

Vespucci: How does *that* work?

Metacult: I'm not exactly sure.

My guess is that a living culture has a way of not being ambiguous. It gives corrections when you make false assumptions about it; that's why people experience culture shock. People trying to re-create a past golden age need never experience culture shock; if you make a false assumption about the golden age, the golden age won't correct you. So the golden age appears to be whatever you want, and people who aren't satisfied with the present, and want to re-create past glory, end up pushing a fantasy that is different both from the present and the past. The Renaissance and Enlightenment neo-classicism both tried to re-create the glory of classical antiquity and are both notable as departures from the past. People who aren't trying to re-create the past can preserve it, saying, "Be gentle with this tradition. It was not inherited from your parents; it is borrowed from your children." People eager to restore past glory all too often, if not sever, severely damage the link between past and future.

I also haven't talked about keeping up with the Trumps, and your unadvertised way to say "No!" to the tyranny of the urgent. I haven't even talked about--

Janra: Stop! Stop. You're going way overboard. He got your point. In fact, I think he got your point half an hour ago. He--

Pater: Could I interrupt for a moment?

Janra: Certainly. What is it?

Pater: I know this is going to sound REALLY strange, but I want a watch.

Vespucci, Janra, Metacult: Huh?

Pater: You heard me.

Janra: But why?

Pater: I know this is going to sound strange, but I want one.

To you a watch represents all sorts of problems, and I don't wonder if you're dumping too much on it. But that's another issue. I don't have the ticking clock in me that you do. There's an issue of sensitivity--I know you hate watches and probably planners, but I burn people by being late and forgetting that just an hour's delay to me is not "just" an hour to them.

Is it really impossible to make a watch that can represent liturgical time, or even hollow out a space liturgical time can abide in? I thought it was possible now to make a watch that will keep track of sunrise and sunset. Scientific engineering can't do some things, but could there be another kind of engineering? I suppose that "even" that technical marvel in your catalogue, the watch that knows how long something feels like, would make an awfully neat conversation piece.

Metacult: I think I may know of just the thing for you.

This watch is a sort of hybrid. Part of it is traditional electronic--something that tells hours, minutes, and seconds, that displays the date, and has a timer, alarm, and a stopwatch accurate to the nearest hundredth of a second--and for that matter it's water resistant to two hundred meters. It's a bit battered--which adds to its masculine look.

But that's not the interesting part. The interesting part has an exquisite sensitivity to liturgical rhythm, such as purely electronic gadgetry could never deliver. And it is a connected time, a part of the Great Dance that moves not according to the wearer's emotions alone but what the Great Choreographer orchestrates. It moves in beautiful ordered time. And there is more. It can enter another person's or place's time, and fit. Among other things.

Pater: This is great! Where can I get one?

Metacult: Just a second while I take off my watch... here's the littlest part. The rest is already inside your heart.

Within the Steel Orb

The car pulled up on the dark cobblestones and stopped by the darker castle. The vehicle was silver-grey, low to the ground, and sleek. A--let us call him a man--opened the driver's door on the right, and stood up, tall, dark, clad in a robe the color of the sky at midnight. Around the car he went, opened the door for his passenger, and once the passenger stepped out, made one swift motion and had two bags on his shoulder. The bags were large, but he moved as if he were accustomed to carrying far heavier fare. It was starlight out, and the moon was visible as moonlight rippled across a pool.

The guest reached for the bags. "Those are heavy. Let me--"

The host smiled darkly. "Do not worry about the weight of your bags."

The host opened a solid greyblack door, of unearthly smoothness, and walked swiftly down a granite hallway, allowing his guest to follow. "You've had a long day. Let me get you something to drink." He turned a door, poured something into two iridescent titanium mugs, and turned through another corridor and opened a door on its side. Inside the room were two deep armchairs and a low table.

"This is my first time traveling behind worlds--how am I to address you?"

The host smiled. "Why do you wish to know more of my

name? It is enough for you to call me Oinos. Please enjoy our welcome."

The guest sipped his drink. "Cider?"

The host said, "You may call it that; it is a juice, which has not had artificial things done to make it taste like it just came out of its fruit regardless of how much it should have aged by the time you taste it. It is juice where time has been allowed to do its work." He was holding a steel orb. "You are welcome here, Art." Then--he barely seemed to move--there was a spark, and Oinos pulled a candle from the wall and set it on the table.

Art said, "Why not a fluorescent light to really light the room up?"

The host said, "For the same reason that you either do not offer your guests mocha at all, or else give them real mocha and not a mix of hot water, instant coffee, and hot cocoa powder. In our world, we can turn the room bright as day any time, but we do not often do so."

"Aah. We have a lot to learn from you about getting back to nature."

"Really? What do you mean by 'getting back to nature'? What do you do to try to 'get back to nature'?"

"Um, I don't know what to really do. Maybe try to be in touch with the trees, not being cooped up inside all the time, if I were doing a better job of it..."

"If that is getting back in touch with nature, then we pay little attention to getting in touch with nature. And nature, as we understand it, is about something fundamentally beyond dancing on hills or sitting and watching waves. I don't criticize you if you do them, but there is really something more. And I can talk with you about drinking juice without touching the natural processes that make cider or what have you, and I can talk with you about natural cycles and why we don't have imitation daylight any time it would seem convenient. But I would like you to walk away with something more, and more interesting, than how we keep technology from being too disruptive to natural processes. That isn't really the point. It's almost what you might call a side effect."

"But you do an awfully impressive job of putting technology in its place and not getting too involved with it."

Oinos said, "Have you had enough chance to stretch out and rest and quench your thirst? Would you like to see something?"

"Yes."

Oinos stood, and led the way down some stairs to a room that seemed to be filled with odd devices. He pushed some things aside, then walked up to a device with a square in the center, and pushed one side. Chains and gears moved, and another square replaced it.

"This is my workshop, with various items that I have worked on. You can come over here and play with this little labyrinth; it's not completely working, but you can explore it if you take the time to figure it out. Come on over. It's what I've been working on most recently."

Art looked around, somewhat amazed, and walked over to the 'labyrinth.'

Oinos said, "In your world, in classical Greek, the same word, 'techne,' means both 'art' and 'technology.' You misunderstand my kindred if you think we aren't especially interested in technology; we have a great interest in technology, as with other kinds of art. But just as you can travel a long distance to see the Mona Lisa without needing a mass-produced Mona Lisa to hang in your bathroom, we enjoy and appreciate technologies without making them conveniences we need to have available every single day."

Art pressed a square and the labyrinth shifted. "Have I come here to see technologies?"

Oinos paused. "I would not advise it. You see our technologies, or how we use them, because that is what you are most ready to see. Visitors from some other worlds hardly notice them, even if they are astonished when they are pointed out."

Art said, "Then why don't we go back to the other room?"

Oinos turned. "Excellent." They went back, and Art sat down in his chair.

Art, after a long pause, said, "I still find it puzzling why, if you appreciate technology, you don't want to have more of it."

Oinos said, "Why do you find it so puzzling?"

"Technology *does* seem to add a lot to the body."

"That is a very misleading way to put it. The effect of most technologies that you think of as adding to the body is in fact to undercut the body. The technologies that you call 'space-conquering' might be appropriately called 'body-conquering.'"

"So the telephone is a body-conquering device? Does it make my body less real?"

"Once upon a time, long ago from your perspective, news and information could not really travel faster than a person could travel. If you were talking with a person, that person had to be pretty close, and it was awkward and inconvenient to communicate with those who were far away. That meant that the people you talked with were probably people from your local community."

"So you were deprived of easy access to people far away?"

"Let me put it this way. It mattered where you were, meaning where your body was. Now, on the telephone, or instant messages, or the web, nothing and no one is really anywhere, and that means profound things for what communities are. And are not. You may have read about 'close-knit rural communities' which have become something exotic and esoteric to most of your world's city dwellers... but when space conquering technologies had not come in, and another space-conquering technology, modern roads allowing easy moving so that people would have to say goodbye to face-to-face friendships every few years... It's a very different way of relating. A close-knit rural community is exotic to you because it is a body-based community in ways that tend not to happen when people make heavy use of body-conquering, or space-conquering, or whatever you want to call them, technologies."

"But isn't there more than a lack of technologies to close-knit communities?"

"Yes, indeed... but... spiritual discipline is about much more than the body, but a lot of spiritual discipline can only shape people when people are running into the body's limitations. The disciplines--worship, prayer, fasting, silence, almsgiving, and so on--only mean something if there are bodily limits you are bumping into. If you can take a pill that takes away your body's discomfort in fasting, or standing through worship, then the body-conquering technology of that pill has cut you off from the spiritual benefit of that practice."

"Aren't spiritual practices about more than the body?"

"Yes indeed, but you won't get there if you have something less than the body."

Art sat back. "I'd be surprised if you're not a real scientist. I imagine that in your world you know things that our scientists will not know for centuries."

Oinos sat back and sat still for a time, closing his eyes. Then he opened his eyes and said, "What have you learned from science?"

"I've spent a lot of time lately, wondering what Einstein's theory of relativity means for us today: even the 'hard' sciences are relative, and what 'reality' is, depends greatly on your own perspective. Even in the hardest sciences, it is fundamentally mistaken to be looking for absolute truth."

Oinos leaned forward, paused, and then tapped the table four different places. In front of Art appeared a gridlike object which Art recognized with a start as a scientific calculator like his son's. "Very well. Let me ask you a question. Relative to your frame of reference, an object of one kilogram rest mass is moving away from you at a speed of one tenth the speed of light. What, from your present frame of reference, is its effective mass?"

Art hesitated, and began to sit up.

Oinos said, "If you'd prefer, the table can be set to function as any major brand of calculator you're familiar with. Or would you prefer a computer with Matlab or Mathematica? The remainder of the table's surface can be used to browse the appropriate manuals."

Art shrunk slightly towards his chair.

Oinos said, "I'll give you hints. In the theory of relativity, objects can have an effective mass of above their rest mass, but never below it. Furthermore, most calculations of this type tend to have anything that changes, change by a factor of the inverse of the square root of the quantity: one minus the square of the object's speed divided by the square of the speed of light. Do you need me to explain the buttons on the calculator?"

Art shrunk into his chair. "I don't know all of those technical details, but I have spent a lot of time thinking about relativity."

Oinos said, "If you are unable to answer that question before I started dropping hints, let alone after I gave hints, you should not pose as having contemplated what relativity means for us today. I'm not trying to humiliate you. But the first question I asked is the kind of question a teacher would put on a quiz to see if students were awake and not playing video games for most of the first lecture. I know it's fashionable in your world to drop Einstein's name as someone you have deeply pondered. It is also extraordinarily silly. I have noticed that scientists who have a good understanding of relativity often work without presenting themselves as having these deep ponderings about what Einstein means for them today. Trying to deeply ponder Einstein without learning even the basics of relativistic physics is like trying to write the next Nobel prize-winning German novel without being bothered to learn even them most rudimentary German vocabulary and grammar."

"But don't you think that relativity makes a big difference?"

"On a poetic level, I think it is an interesting development in your world's history for a breakthrough in science, Einstein's theory of relativity, to say that what is absolute is not time, but light. Space and time bend before light. There is a poetic beauty to Einstein making an unprecedented absolute out of light. But let us leave poetic appreciation of Einstein's theory aside.

"You might be interested to know that the differences predicted by Einstein's theory of relativity are so minute that decades passed between Einstein making the theory of relativity and people being able to use a sensitive enough clock to measure the minute difference of the so-called 'twins paradox' by bringing an atomic clock on an airplane. The answer to the problem I gave you is that for a tenth the speed of light--which is faster than you can imagine, and well over a thousand times the top speed of the fastest supersonic vehicle your world will ever make--is one half of one percent. It's a disappointingly small increase for a rather astounding speed. If the supersonic Skylon is ever built, would you care to guess the increase in effective mass as it travels at an astounding Mach 5.5?"

"Um, I don't know..."

"Can you guess? Half its mass? The mass of a car? Or just the mass of a normal-sized adult?"

"Is this a trick question? Fifty pounds?"

"The effective mass increases above the rest mass, for that massive vehicle running at about five times the speed of sound and almost twice the top speed of the SR-71 Blackbird, is something like the mass of a mosquito."

"A *mosquito*? You're joking, right?"

"No. It's an underwhelming, *microscopic* difference for what relativity says when the rumor mill has it that Einstein taught us that hard sciences are as fuzzy as anything else... or that perhaps, in Star Wars terms, 'Luke, you're going to find that many of the truths we cling to depend greatly on your own point of view.' Under Einstein, you will in fact **not** find that many of the observations that we cling to, depend greatly on your own frame of reference. You have to be doing something pretty exotic to have relativity make any measurable difference from the older physics at all."

"Would you explain relativity to me so that I can discuss its implications?"

"I really think there might be more productive ways to use your visit."

"But you have a scientist's understanding of relativity."

"I am not sure I'd say that."

"Why? You seem to understand relativity a lot more like a scientist than I do."

"Let's talk about biology for a moment. Do you remember the theory of spontaneous generation? You know, the theory that life just emerges from appropriate material?"

"I think so."

"But your world's scientists haven't believed in spontaneous generation since over a century before you were born. Why would you be taught that theory--I'm assuming you learned this in a science class and not digging into history'?"

"My science course explained the theory in covering historical background, even though scientists no longer believe that bread spontaneously generates mold."

"Let me ask what may seem like a non-sequitur. I assume you're familiar with people who are working to get even more of religion taken out of public schools?"

"Yes."

"They are very concerned about official prayers at school events, right? About having schools endorse even the occasional religious practice?"

"Yes."

"Ok. Let me ask what may seem like a strange question. Have these 'separation of Church and state' advocates also advocated that geometry be taken out of the classroom?"

Art closed his eyes, and then looked at Oinos as if he had two heads. "It seems you don't know everything about my world."

"I don't. But please understand that geometry did not originate as a secular technical practice. You migth have heard this mentioned. Geometry began its life as a 'sacred science,' or a religious practice, and to its founders the idea that geometry does not have religious content would have struck them as worse than saying that prayer does not have religious content."

"Ok, I think I remember that being mentioned. So to speak, my math teacher taught about geometry the 'sacred science' the way that my biology teacher taught about the past theory of spontaneous generation."

Oinos focused his eyes on Art. "In our schools, and in our training, physics, biology, and chemistry are 'taught' as 'secular sciences' the same way, in your school, spontaneous generation is taught as 'past science', or even better, the 'sacred science' of geometry is 'taught' in the course of getting on to a modern understanding of geometry."

Art said, "So the idea that the terrain we call 'biology' is to you--"

Oinos continued: "As much something peered at through a glass bell as the idea that the terrain of regular polygons belongs to a secularized mathematics."

"What is a sacred science?"

Oinos sat back. "If a science is about understanding something as self-contained whose explanations do not involve God, and it is an attempt to understand as physics understand, and the scientist understands as a detached observer, looking in through a window, then you have a secular science--the kind that reeks of the occult to us. Or that may sound strange, because in your world people proclaiming sacred sciences are proclaiming the occult. But let me deal with that later. A sacred science does not try to understand objects as something that can be explained without reference to God. A sacred science is first and foremost about God, not about objects. When it understands objects, it understands them out of God, and tries to see God shining through them. A sacred science has its home base in the understanding of God, not of inanimate matter, and its understanding of things bears the imprint of God. If you want the nature of its knowing in an image, do not think of someone looking in and observing, detached, through a window, but someone drinking something in."

"Is everything a sacred science to you? And what is a sacred science? Astrology?"

"Something like that, except that I use the term 'sacred science' by way of accommodation. Our own term is one that has no good translation in your language. But let us turn to the stars."

"Astrology is right in this: a star is more than a ball of plasma. Even in the Bible there is not always such a distinction between the ranks of angels and the stars as someone raised on materialist science might think." He rose, and began to walk, gesturing for Art to follow him. In the passage, they turned and entered a door. Oinos lit a lamp next to an icon on the wall.

The icon looked like starlight. It showed angels praying at the left, and then the studded sapphiric canopy of the night sky behind a land with herbs shooting from the earth, and on the right an immense Man--if he was a Man--standing, his hand raised in benediction. All around the sapphire dome were some majestic figures, soaring aloft in two of their six wings. Art paused to drink it in.

"What are those symbols?"

"They are Greek letters. You are looking at an icon of the creation of the stars, but the text is not the text for that day; it is from another book, telling of the angels thunderously shouting for joy when the stars were created. So the stars are connected with the angels."

"Is this astrology?"

"No, because the stars and angels both point to God. The influences in astrology point beyond matter to something else, but they do not point far enough beyond themselves. If you can use something to make a forecast that way, it doesn't point far enough beyond itself."

"Why not?"

"One definition to distinguish religion from magic--one used by anthropologists--is that religion is trying to come into contact with the divine, and magic is trying to control the divine. God cannot be controlled, and there is something of control in trying to foretell a future that God holds in mystery. A real God cannot be pried into by a skill. Astrology departs from a science that can only see stars as so much plasma, but it doesn't go far enough to lead people to look into the stars and see a shadow of their Creator. To be a sacred science, it is not enough to point to something more than matter as secular science understands it; as the term is used in our language, one can only be a *sacred* science by pointing to God."

"Then what is a sacred science? Which branches of learning

as you break them up? Can they even be translated into my language?"

"You seem to think that if astrology is not a sacred science then sacred sciences must be something much more hidden. Not so. Farming is a sacred science, as is hunting, or inventing, or writing. When a monk makes incense, it is not about how much incense he can make per unit of time; his making incense is the active part of living contemplatively, and his prayer shows itself in physical labor. His act is more than material production; it is a sacred science, or sacred art or sacred endeavor, and what goes into and what comes out of the activity is prayer. Nor is it simply a matter that he is praying while he acts; his prayers matter for the incense. There are many lands from your world's Desert Fathers to Mexico in your own day where people have a sense that it matters what state people cook in, and that cooking with love puts something into a dish that no money can buy. Perhaps you will not look at me askance when I say that not only monks in their monasteries exotically making incense for worship are performing a sacred science, but cooking, for people who may be low on the totem pole and who are not considered exotic, as much as for anyone else, can and should be a sacred science. Like the great work that will stay up with a sick child all night."

"Hmm..." Art said, and then finished his tankard. "Have you traveled much?"

"I have not reached one in five of the galaxies with inhabited worlds. I can introduce you to people who have some traveling experience, but I am not an experienced traveler. Still, I have met sites worth visiting. I have met, learned, worshiped. Traveling in this castle I have drunk the blood of gems. There are worlds where there is nothing to see, for all is music, and song does everything that words do for you. I have beheld a star as it formed, and I have been part of an invention that moves forward as a thousand races in their laboratories add their devices. I have read books, and what is more I have spoken with members of different worlds and races. There seems to be no shortage of wonders, and I have even been to your own world, with people who write fantasy that continues to astonish us--"

"My son-in-law is big into fantasy--he got me to see a Lord of the whatever-it-was movie--but I don't fancy them much myself."

"We know about Tolkein, but he is not considered a source of astonishing fantasy to us."

"Um..." Art took a long time to recall a name, and Oinos waited patiently. "Lewis?"

"If you're looking for names you would have heard of, Voltaire and Jung are two of the fantasy authors we consider essential. Tolkein and Lewis are merely imaginative. It is Voltaire and Jung who are truly fantasy authors. But there are innumerable others in your world."

Art said, "Um... what do you mean by 'fantasy author'?"

Oinos turned. "I'm sorry; there is a discrepancy between how your language uses 'fantasy author' and ours. We have two separate words that your 'fantasy' translates, and the words stand for very different concepts. One refers to works of imagination that are set in another world that is not confused with reality. The other refers to a fundamental confusion that can cost a terrible price. Our world does not produce fiction; we do appreciate the fiction of other worlds, but we do not draw a particularly strong line between fiction where only the characters and events are imagined, and fiction where the whole world is imagined. But we do pay considerable attention to the second kind of fantasy, and our study of fantasy authors is not a study of imagination but a study of works that lead people into unreality. 'Fantasy author' is one of the more important terms in understanding your world and its history."

Art failed to conceal his reaction.

"Or perhaps I was being too blunt. But, unfashionable as it may be, there is such a thing as evil in your world, and the ways in which people live, including what they believe, has something to do with it. Not everything, but something."

Oinos waited for a time. Then, when Art remained silent, he said, "Come with me. I have something to show you." He opened a door on the other side of the room, and went into the next room. The room was lit by diffuse moonlight, and there was a ledge around the room and water which Oinos stirred with his hand to light a phosphorescent glow. When Art had stepped in, Oinos stepped up, balancing on a steel cable, and stood silent for a while. "Is there anything here that you can focus on?"

"What do you mean?"

"Step up on this cable and take my hand."

"What if I fall into the water?"

Art tried to balance, but it seemed even more difficult in the dark. For a while, he tried to keep his balance with Oinos's help, but he seemed barely up. He overcompensated twice in opposite directions, began flying into the water, and was stopped at last by Oinos's grip, strong as steel, on his arm.

"I can't do this," Art said.

"Very well." Oinos opened a door on the other side of the room, and slowly led him out. As they walked, Oinos started up a spiral staircase and sat down to rest after Art reached the top. Then Art looked up at the sky, and down to see what looked like a telescope.

"What is it?"

"A telescope, not too different from those of your world."

Oinos stood up, looked at it, and began some adjustments. Then he called Art over, and said, "Do you see that body?"

"What is it?"

"A small moon."

Oinos said, "I want you to look at it as closely as you can," and then pulled something on the telescope.

"It's moving out of sight."

"That's right; I just deactivated the tracking feature. You should be able to feel handles; you can move the telescope with them."

"Why do I need to move the telescope? Is the moon moving?"

"This planet is rotating: what the telescope sees will change as it rotates with the planet, and on a telescope you can see the rotation."

Art moved the handles and found that it seemed either not to move at all or else move a lot when he put pressure on it.

Art said, "This is a hard telescope to control."

Oinos said, "The telescope is worth controlling."

"Can you turn the tracking back on?"

Oinos merely repeated, "The telescope is worth controlling."

The celestial body had moved out of view. Art made several movements, barely passed over the moon, and then found it. He tried to see what he could, then give a relatively violent shove when the moon reached the edge of his field of view, and see if he could observe the body that way. After several tries, he began to get the object consistently in view... and found that he was seeing the same things about it, not being settled enough between jolts to really focus on what was there.

Art tried to make a smooth, slow movement with his body, and found that a much taller order than it sounded. His movement, which he could have sworn was gentle and smooth, produced what seemed like erratic movement, and it was only with greatest difficulty that he held the moon in view.

"Is this badly lubricated? Or do you have lubrication in this world?"

"We do, on some of our less precise machines. This telescope is massive, but it's not something that moves roughly when it is pushed smoothly; the joints move so smoothly that putting oil or other lubricants that are familiar to you would make them move much more roughly."

"Then why is it moving roughly every time I push it smoothly?"

"Maybe you aren't pushing it as smoothly as you think you are?"

Art pushed back his irritation, and then found the moon again. And found, to his dismay, that when the telescope jerked, he had moved the slightest amount unevenly.

Art pushed observation of the moon to the back of his mind.

He wanted to move the telescope smoothly enough that he wouldn't have to keep finding the moon again. After a while, he found that this was less difficult than he thought, and tried for something harder: keeping the moon in the center of what he could see in the telescope.

He found, after a while, that he could keep the moon in the center if he tried, and for periods was able to manage something even harder: keeping the moon from moving, or perhaps just moving slowly. And then, after a time, he found himself concentrating through the telescope on taking in the beauty of the moon.

It was breathtaking, and Art later could never remember a time he had looked on something with quite that fascination.

Then Art realized he was exhausted, and began to sit down; Oinos pulled him to a bench.

After closing his eyes for a while, Art said, "This was a magnificent break from your teaching."

"A break from teaching? What would you mean?"

Art sat, opened his mouth, and then closed it. After a while, he said, "I was thinking about what you said about fantasy authors... do you think there is anything that can help?"

Oinos said, "Let me show you." He led Art into a long corridor with smooth walls and a round arch at top. A faint blue glow followed them, vanishing at the edges. Art said, "Do you think it will be long before our world has full artificial intelligence?"

Oinos said, "Hmm... Programming artificial intelligence on a computer is not *that* much more complex than getting a stone to lay an egg."

Art said, "But our scientists are making progress. Your advanced world has artificial intelligence, right?"

Oinos said, "Why on earth would we be able to do that? Why would that even be a goal?"

"You have computers, right?"

"Yes, indeed; the table that I used to call up a scientific calculator works on the same principle as your world's computers.

I could almost say that inventing a new kind of computer is a rite of passage among serious inventors, or at least that's the closest term your world would have."

"And your computer science is pretty advanced, right? Much more advanced than ours?"

"We know things that the trajectory of computer science in your world will never reach because it is not pointed in the right direction." Oinos tapped the wall and arcs of pale blue light spun out.

"Then you should be well beyond the point of making artificial intelligence."

"Why on a million, million worlds should we ever be able to do that? Or even think that is something we *could* accomplish?"

"Well, if I can be obvious, the brain is a computer, and the mind is its software."

"Is it?"

"What else could the mind be?"

"What else could the mind be? What about an altar at which to worship? A workshop? A bridge between Heaven and earth, a meeting place where eternity meets time? A treasury in which to gather riches? A spark of divine fire? A line in a strong grid? A river, ever flowing, ever full? A tree reaching to Heaven while its roots grasp the earth? A mountain made immovable for the greatest storm? A home in which to live and a ship by which to sail? A constellation of stars? A temple that sanctifies the earth? A force to draw things in? A captain directing a starship or a voyager who can travel without? A diamond forged over aeons from of old? A perpetual motion machine that is simply impossible but functions anyway? A faithful manuscript by which an ancient book passes on? A showcase of holy icons? A mirror, clear or clouded? A wind which can never be pinned down? A haunting moment? A home with which to welcome others, and a mouth with which to kiss? A strand of a web? An acrobat balancing for his whole life long on a slender crystalline prism between two chasms? A protecting veil and a concealing mist? An eye to glimpse the uncreated Light as the world moves on its way? A rift yawning into the depths of the earth? A kairometer, both primeval and young? A--"

"All right, all right! I get the idea, and that's some pretty lovely poetry. (What's a kairometer?) These are all very beautiful metaphors for the mind, but I am interested in what the mind is literally."

"Then it might interest you to hear that your world's computer is also a metaphor for the mind. A good and poetic metaphor, perhaps, but a metaphor, and one that is better to balance with other complementary metaphors. It is the habit of some in your world to understand the human mind through the metaphor of the latest technology for you to be infatuated with. Today, the mind is a computer, or something like that. Before you had the computer, 'You're just wired that way' because the brain or the mind or whatever is a wired-up telephone exchange, the telephone exchange being your previous object of technological infatuation, before the computer. Admittedly, 'the mind is a computer' is an attractive metaphor. But there is some fundamental confusion in taking *that* metaphor literally and assuming that, since the mind is a computer, all you have to do is make some more progress with technology and research and you can give a computer an intelligent mind."

"I know that computers don't have emotions yet, but they seem to have rationality down cold."

"Do they?"

"Are you actually going to tell me that computers, with their math and logic, aren't rational?"

"Let me ask you a question. Would you say that the thing you can hold, a thing that you call a book, can make an argument?"

"Yes; I've seen some pretty good ones."

"Really? How do paper and ink think out their position?"

Art hesitated, and said, "Um, if you're going to nitpick..."

"I'm not nitpicking. A book is a tool of intelligent communication, and they are part of how people read author's stories, or explanation of how to do things, or poetry, or ideas. But the physical thing is not thereby intelligent. However much you think of a book as making an argument, the book is incapable of knowing what an argument is, and for that matter the paper and ink have no idea of whether they contain the world's best classic, or something mediocre, or incoherent accusations that world leaders are secretly planning to turn your world to dog drool, or randomly generated material that is absolute gibberish. The book may be meaningful to you, but the paper with ink on it is not the sort of thing that can understand what you recognize through the book.

"This might ordinarily be nitpicking, but it says something important about computers. One of the most difficult things for computer science instructors in your world to pound through people's heads is that a computer does not get the gist of what you are asking it to do and overlook minor mistakes, because the computer has no sense of what you are doing and no way to discern what were trying to get it to do from a mistake where you wrote in a bug by telling it to do something slightly different from what you meant. The computer has no sense that a programmer meant anything. A computer follows instructions, one after another, whether or not they make sense, and indeed without being able to wonder whether they make sense. To you, a program may be a tool that acts as an electronic shopping cart to let you order things through the web, but the web server no more understands that it is being used as a web server than a humor book understands that it is meant to make people laugh. Now most or all of the books you see are meant to say something--there's not much market for a paperback volume filled with random gibberish--but a computer can't understand that it is running a program written for a purpose any more than a book can understand that the ink on its pages is intended for people to read."

Art said, "You don't think artificial intelligence is making real progress? They seem to keep making new achievements."

Oinos said, "The rhetoric of 'We're making real

breakthroughs now; we're on the verge of full artificial intelligence, and with what we're achieving, full artificial intelligence is just around the corner' is not new: people have been saying that full artificial intelligence is just around the corner since before you were born. But *breeding a better and better kind of apple tree is not progress towards growing oranges.* Computer science, and not just artificial intelligence, has gotten good at getting computers to function better as computers. But human intelligence is something else... and it is profoundly missing the point to only realize that the computer is missing a crucial ingredient of the most computer-like activity of human rational analysis. Even if asking a computer to recognize a program's purpose reflects a fundamental error--you're barking up the wrong telephone pole. Some people from your world say that when you have a hammer, everything begins to look like a nail. The most interesting thing about the mind is not that it can do something more complete when it pounds in computer-style nails. It's something else entirely."

"But what?"

"When things are going well, the 'computer' that performs calculating analysis is like your moon: a satellite, that reflects light from something greater. Its light is useful, but there is something more to be had. The sun, as it were, is that the mind is like an altar, or even something better. It takes long struggles and work, but you need to understand that the heart of the mind is at once practical and spiritual, and that its greatest fruit comes not in speech but in silence."

Art was silent for a long time.

Oinos stopped, tapped a wall once, and waited as an opening appeared in the black stone. Inside an alcove was a small piece of rough hewn obsidian; Oinos reached in, took it, and turned it to reveal another side, finely machined, with a series of concentric ridged grooves centered around a tiny niche. "You asked what a kairometer was, and this is a kairometer, although it would take you some time to understand exactly what it is."

"Is it one of the other types of computers in your world?"

"Yes. I would call it information technology, although not like the information technology you know. It is something people come back to, something by which people get something more than they had, but it does this not so much according to its current state as to our state in the moment we are using it. It does not change." Oinos placed the object in Art's hands.

Art slowly turned it. "Will our world have anything like this?"

Oinos took the kairometer back and returned it to its niche; when he withdrew his hand, the opening closed with a faint whine. "I will leave you to find that yourself."

Oinos began walking, and they soon reached the end of the corridor. Art followed Oinos through the doorway at the end and gasped.

Through the doorway was something that left Art trying to figure out whether or not it was a room. It was a massive place, lit by a crystalline blue light. As Art looked around, he began to make sense of his surroundings: there were some bright things, lower down, in an immense room with rounded arches and a dome at the top, made of pure glass. Starlight streamed in. Art stepped through the doorway and sunk down a couple of inches.

Oinos stooped for a moment, and then said, "Take off your shoes. They are not needed here." Art did so, and found that he was walking on a floor of velveteen softness. In the far heart of the room a thin plume of smoke arose. Art could not tell whether he smelled a fragrance, but he realized there was a piercing chant. Art asked, "What is the chant saying?"

Oinos did not answer.

What was the occasion? Art continued to look, to listen, and began trying to drink it in. It almost sounded as if they were preparing to receive a person of considerable importance. There was majesty in the air.

Oinos seemed to have slipped away.

Art turned and saw an icon behind him, hanging on the glass. There was something about it he couldn't describe. The icon was dark, and the colors were bright, almost luminous. A man lay dreaming at the bottom, and something reached up to a light hidden in the clouds--was it a ladder? Art told himself the artistic effect was impressive, but there was something that seemed amiss in that way of looking at it.

What bothered him about saying the icon had good artistic effect? Was the artistry bad? That didn't seem to be it. He looked at a couple of areas of artistic technique, but it was difficult to do so; such analysis felt like a foreign intrusion. He thought about his mood, but that seemed to be the wrong place to look, and almost the same kind of intrusion. There seemed to be something shining through the icon; looking at it was like other things he had done in this world, only moreso. He was looking through the icon and not around it, but... Art had some sense of what it was, but it was not something he could fit into words.

After being absorbed in the icon, Art looked around. There must have been hundreds of icons around, and lights, and people; he saw what seemed like a sparse number of people--of Oinos's kind--spread out through the vast space. There was a chant of some kind that changed from time to time, but seemed to somehow be part of the same flow. Things seemed to move very slowly--or move in a different time, as if clock time were turned on its side, or perhaps as if he had known clock time as it was turned on its side and now it was right side up--but Art never had the sense of nothing going on. There seemed to always be something more going on than he could grasp.

Art shifted about, having stood for what seemed like too long, sat down for a time, and stood up. The place seemed chaotic, in a way cluttered, yet when he looked at the "clutter," there was something shining through, clean as ice, majestic as starlight, resonant as silence, full of life as the power beneath the surface of a river, and ordered with an order that no rectangular grid could match. He did not understand any of the details of the brilliant dazzling darkness... but they spoke to him none the less.

After long hours of listening to the chant, Art realized with a start that the fingers of dawn had stolen all around him, and he saw stone and verdant forest about the glass walls until the sunlight began to blaze. He thought, he though he could understand the song even as its words remained beyond his reach, and he wished the light would grow stronger so he could see more. There was a crescendo all about him, and--

Oinos was before him. Perhaps for some time.

"I almost understand it," Art said. "I have started to taste this world."

Oinos bowed deeply. "It is time for you to leave."

The Steel Orb

I awoke, seared by pain. The images dispersed. What were they?

a flat rectangular courtyard, where brick pillars enshrined a walkway, and in the center was a great pool, filled not with water but with silt impressed with intricate patterns--a place that was silent and still, cool in the shade, with robed men moving slowly and conversing without breaking the stillness

alleys and courtyards and tunnels and passageways that made for a labyrinth, with a byzantine structure only exceeded by turgid forms beneath its surface--I was moving through it before I had grasped its rhythm

a vortex, draining life and beauty, draining the life out of--

there was also a single grain of incense, its fragrance filling--

there had been a storm, with wind and water and lightning moving faster than I could keep pace with, a storm, a storm--

then I awoke.

I had washed up on a beach, barely conscious, torn by thirst. I did not see the city in the distance; I saw only a man, clad in a deep blue robe. I tried to call out to him, but I was torn by violent coughs.

Then the scene blurred, and I passed out of consciousness.

When I regained consciousness, I was in a room. There was

a man whose hand was on my heart; he looked familiar, I thought. A woman handed him a cup, which he placed to my lips.

Time passed. I could feel warmth and coolness moving through me. My thoughts slowly quickened. He reverenced me, making on himself the great sign, bowing, and kissing me. I went to stand, but he held me down. "Take a time of rest now. In a day I will introduce you to the city."

I looked at him. The blue robe looked familiar. A question did not arise in my mind; I only wondered later that I did not ask if he had been expecting me, or if he knew I wanted to be a Teacher. Something in his repose kept the question from arising.

The woman looked at me briefly. "My name is Pool. What languages do you know?"

If anything, I sank further back into my chair. I wished the question would go away. When she continued to listen, I waited for sluggish thoughts to congeal. "I... Fish, Shroud, Inscription, and Shadow are all languages that are spoken around my island, and I speak all of them well. I speak Starlight badly, despite the fact that they trade with our village frequently. I do not speak Stream well at all, even though it is known to many races of voyagers. I once translated a book from Boulder to Pedestal, although that is hardly to be reckoned: it was obscure and technical, and it has nothing of the invisible subtlety of 'common' conversation. You know how--"

The man said, "Yes; something highly technical in a matter you understand is always easier to translate than children's talk. Go on."

"And--I created a special purpose language," I said, "to try to help a child who couldn't speak. I did my best, but it didn't work. I still don't understand why not. And I--" I tried to think, to remember if there were any languages I had omitted. Nothing returned to my mind.

I looked down and closed my eyes. "I'm sorry. I'm not very good with languages."

The woman spoke, and when I looked up I noticed her green veil and the beautiful wrinkles about her eyes. "You novices think you know nothing and need to know everything. When I was near your point in life, I knew only six tongues, and I'm still only fluent in four." She reverenced me, then stepped out the window. Her husband followed, although their spirits still seemed to blow in the wind through the window.

I fell into a deep and dreamless sleep, and I awoke with a start. The man was just stepping into the window, and I could hear a clink of silver. "Will you come to the marketplace? I want you to find the Galleria."

He still had not told me his name, nor I mine, but as we walked, I told him about the great storm; it was wild on land but wilder at sea. He wondered that I survived the storm, let alone that I washed up; he quoted the proverb, "Where the wind blows, no one knows." We came to a merchant with dried fruits; he looked at some oranges. "Have you seen Book since you came back?"

"Yes, but I didn't get to talk with him long."

"What did he say?"

"He only said two things. The first was, 'Put my little daughter down!' Then the second was... let me see if I can remember. He began to say, 'No, don't throw her in the--' But I couldn't hear the rest of what he hoped to say, because he threw a bucket of salt water at me. Which reminds me, I don't have salted fish today, but I have some of the finest oranges from the four corners of the world. This orange grew in an orchard where it is said that the trees once bore jewels. I could sell you this fine assortment for two silver pieces each."

My host sounded astonished. "Two silver pieces each? You are a dear friend, of much more value than the wares you sell. I doubt if you paid two silver pieces for this whole lot of fruit--look at this one! It must have rotted before it was dried. I can talk a bit, but I'm only buying wheat today." He turned away.

The merchant grabbed his arm. "Don't go yet. I'll give you a friend's price." I think he said something else impressive, but their haggling could not hold my interest. The market was pungent with strange smells. I recognised the smell of spices, but what else was there? Something strange. I could hear a tantalizing sound of gears, but that was not it. There was a soft sound of wind. What was evading my mind?

I realised my host was walking, holding a bag with some dried oranges. I hastened to follow him.

"My name is Fortress," he said.

"I am Unspoken."

"Unspoken... That's an ambiguous name. You seem to be shrouded in mystery. Have you seen the Galleria?"

We stopped in the Temple, drinking the flow of chant and incense, and reverencing the holy icons. Then we walked out. Fortress showed me a hedge maze in a public park, with a great statue in the centre. I looked at the pedestal, and something caught my eye. "There's a passage down hidden in the pedestal to the statue. Where does it go?"

He laughed. "You're subtle."

I waited for him to continue.

He remained silent.

I asked him, "Will it help me find the Galleria?"

He said, "It helps me find the Galleria. It will only distract you from it. The far wall of the pedestal opens to a passage down, but it only reaches a network of caves where boys play. There is nothing in there that will interest you."

"Then what," I asked, "am I to do to find the Galleria?"

"Why don't you search? The Galleria is not outside the boundaries of this little labyrinth. Only beware of the first solution you want to latch onto. That is often a distraction, and if you are to find a solution you are looking for, you need to be able to grasp something slippery in a place you are not looking."

I knocked on earth with my ear to the ground; I looked at the cracks between stones; I even scraped a piece of chalk someone had left on the stones, trying to see if its trace would show me a different stone. I found a few loose items; someone had forgotten a brush, and I pushed a lot of earth aside. I searched and searched, but I found no sign of a passage, no sign of anything unusual save the echoes of a hollow shaft in the stone beneath the statue. It was easy for me to find the mechanism to open the pedestal; indeed, I saw a boy emerge from it. I looked around near the statue: could I be missing a second passage nearby? Yet here the search was even more frustrating.

Fortress gave me a slice of orange, and I searched, hot, parched, the whole day through. I was near the point of tears; nothing in the ground offered the faintest trace of a way down.

I sat back in desolation. I rested my back against a hedge; I could see the sleepy sun's long golden fingers sliding across the hedge. I closed my eyes for a few minutes to rest; I opened my eyes, and could see that the sun's fingers had shifted. My bleak eyes rested on a funny bulge in the hedge. That was odd; it looked almost as if--I stared. Standing out from the hedge, illuminated in stark relief, was a bas-relief sculpture.

Someone in a robe--what color robe?--swam in the ocean. He swam down, down, down, down, deeper than a whale can dive, and still deeper. Something about the picture filled me with cool, and I began to see through it, began to see the web that it was--I felt a touch on my head. "You've found the Galleria. Would you like to go home now?"

I looked. Past Fortress I saw another picture of a swordsman wielding the great Sword, slicing through darkness and error. The Sword swung around him, slicing through monsters around him, and then with no less force slicing through the monsters inside him. I could see--what? It hurt him to cut at errors inside him, but he wielded the Sword against the darkness without and within. I looked entranced.

"Stand up." Fortress was looking at me. "You've seen enough for now; I normally only look into one picture, and you have looked into two after finding the entrance into the Galleria. We will see more of the city later; now, you are tired."

It wasn't until I began walking home that I realized how exhausted I was. I ate my meal in silence, lay in my bed, and sunk into sleep. I awoke, still tired, and was relieved when Fortress told me that he had one proper lesson for me but he would need several days' mundane work for me after that, and it would be a while before anything else exciting happened.

There was one workroom, one that had a forge, an unstable stack of cups with gears and levers, and a box of silt for drawing. There were several mechanical devices in various states of disassembly; Fortress picked up one of them, and turned a crank. I could see gears turning, but the white bird on top moved very erratically.

Fortress looked at me. "Does it work?"

"Not very well."

"What part is causing the problem?"

I turned the device over in my hands, pushed and pulled at one axle, and turned the crank. After some time, I said, "This gear here isn't connecting. It's worn and small."

"So if I replace that gear, it will work better?"

I hesitated and said, "No."

"Then what is the problem?"

"The entire device is loose. The teeth aren't really close enough anywhere; there's room for slipping."

"Then is that one gear the problem?"

"No. It is only the easiest thing to blame."

"Then you did not help yourself or me by telling me that it was that one gear."

I opened my mouth to protest, but he held up his hand and said, "People will often ask you treacherous questions like that, and they usually won't know what it is that they're doing. A Teacher, such as you seem to want to be--"

"How did you know I wanted to be a Teacher?"

"How could I not know you wanted to be a Teacher? A Teacher, such as you seem to want to be--" he continued, "gives an answer that will help the other person, even if that answer is not expected, even if the other person doesn't want to hear it."

Fortress shook the clockwork and said, "What would make it work?"

I said, "You could replace all the gear heads with something larger?"

He said, "What if you couldn't do that? What if the gear

heads were made of delicately crafted gold?"

I hesitated, and said, "I can't think of anything that would help."

"Anything at all?"

I hesitated again, and said, "If you made the casing smaller, it would work. But how would you--"

He reached down and pulled two metal plates, plus some other hardware and tools, setting them before me. I took the tools, disassembled the original device, and reassembled the new device with a slightly smaller frame.

It worked perfectly.

He asked, "Is there any way for the bird to bob up and down, as well as turn?"

I tried to think of how to answer him, but this time I really could think of nothing. My sense of mental balance, my sense that my understanding was big enough to encompass his Lesson, was wavery. I was unsure.

He took a metal rule, and smoothed the surface of the silt inside the box. He then began drawing with a stylus.

"What if the rod were not solid, but had a cam and inner workings like this? Wouldn't that work?"

I looked at him, slightly dazed. "You must be a great metalworker. Can you do that?"

He paused a moment and said, "I might be a great metalworker, and I might be able to do that, but that is not why I am asking. Would it work?"

"Yes."

"Could you make it roll?"

"Yes. Put it in a hollow round casing and then it would roll as part of the casing."

He laughed and said, "Could you have the front move forward and the back stay in place--without it breaking?"

I cleared the silt's surface, and began to work diagrams--rejecting several as they failed, working one almost to completion--and then saying, "But that would require a shell that is both strong and elastic, and I have not heard of any who can make a shell like that."

He seemed unconcerned. "But would it work?"

"If I had such a shell, yes, it would work."

"Then you have created it. Could you make one that gives birth to another like itself?"

I sketched a descending abyss of machines within machines, each one smaller than its parent.

"Could you make one that gives birth to another machine, just like itself?"

"Yes, if they were all constantly expanding. By the time a child gave birth, it would be the size of its parent when the child gave birth."

He seemed impressed, not only at what I said, but at how quickly. He closed his eyes, and said, "I will only ask you one more question. How would you design a machine that could design machines like itself?"

I looked at him, at the disassembled machines, at the silt, and then to a place inside myself. "I can't, and I can't learn now."

He looked at me, opened his mouth, and closed it. He said, "We can move to another Lesson. For now, I want you to look at the gears, separating the worn ones from the ones that are new, so that I can melt down the worn ones. You've got a meticulous day ahead of you."

He left, and I began to work through the gears. The work began to grow monotonous. He returned with a leather sack over his shoulder. "I just acquired a number of broken clockwork devices which I want you to disassemble and separate into parts that are usable and parts that need to be melted down. I'll be back shortly with some metal to melt down and forge new gears out of." He set down the sack, and I looked in disbelief at the intricate machines with innumerable small parts. I had a bleak sense of how long a stretch of dullness was ahead of me. I started to lay them out so I could disassemble them.

He returned, holding a pike in his hands. "You seem strong, and you've had some time to recover. Come with me. Thunder has spotted a bear."

Fortress stood, armed with a sword, a crossbow, and several quarrels. He had given the pike to me; we followed several other men and spread out into the woods. Fortress told me, "I want you just to search, and cry out if you see the bear--we'll come. Don't attack the bear; just set the pike if it charges, and run once it's hit. I think you have a good chance of noticing the bear. Don't take any unnecessary risks."

We spread out, and I moved along, my feet slipping noiselessly on the forest soil. It was more of an effort than it should have been; my body seemed to move with all the fluidity of sludge. The forest looked more rugged than usual; the storm which almost killed me had torn through the forest, and the storm's mark was far heavier on the forest than the city. I thought of the saying that a storm is liquid fire.

I looked at a tree that had fallen. The dead tree had broken a branch on another tree, and left an unpleasant wound. I cut the hanging branch with my pike, to leave better wound. Then I placed my hand on the tree to bless it, and left it to heal.

I thought of how the hunt would go. Someone would see it, then the men would gather. Those the bear faced away from would fire a volley of arrows. Those it chased would run while others taunted it. When the hunters left the city, there was an edge of excitement; I don't think it would be the same if it were not risky.

I continued to move along noiselessly, and looked for a creek. I was thirsty. I blessed another tree, hoping it would heal: the storm had left some rather impressive wreckage. It was dead silent, and when I cut a damaged branch from a third tree, two things happened. First, I heard a babbling brook, and realized how parched I was. Second, part of my pike caught on the tree, and I couldn't wrest it free.

Leaving the pike for a moment, I stole away from the tree and refreshed myself at the brook. I sat for a moment and rested, breathing in simple joy. Then I heard a stick snap on the other side of a rocky outcropping. I realised I could hear some very loud pawprints.

I slithered up the rock, and looked around. I saw nothing.

Then I looked down, and saw the biggest bear of my life.

It looked around.

It smelled.

I held tight against the rock.

Something under my right hand moved noiselessly. My fingers wrapped around a large stone, the size of a man's skull.

Fear flowed through me. And excitement. I lifted the rock, slowly, noiselessly, and brought my legs in. I lifted the rock.

I felt with my left hand, and found a rock the thickness of my wrist. A flick of my wrist, and it crashed thirty cubits away.

The bear turned its head, and began to run.

As it ran, I jumped.

I began to fall.

I could see the forest moving as if it had almost stopped.

Between every beat of my heart, a thousand things happened.

I landed on the bear's back, astride it as if I were riding it.

Immediately the bear tensed, and began to turn.

The rock, still in my hand, crushed the bear's skull.

I could hear a crunch, and the bear's body suddenly went limp.

My hand released the stone.

The stone began to fall, about to roll over on my leg and crush me.

My hand caught a thin branch from a tree.

I pulled my legs up and pulled the branch as hard as I could.

I tore it off.

The bear's body turned.

Something slapped my other palm.

I pulled with all my strength, and my body lifted from the bear.

The bear hit the ground.

I looked around.

Most hunting parties killed a bear every few years.

I had heard of a warrior who had killed a bear alone.

I had never heard of someone kill a bear with only the weapons the forest provided.

I lowered myself to the ground.

I watched the bear breathe its last.

I shouted with a roar like a storm's fury.

Other men began to arrive. Their jaws dropped when they saw me standing over the bear's carcass--empty-handed.

Fortress walked up to me.

I smiled, with a smile of exhilaration such as I had never smiled before.

He looked into me, looked at all the other men, then curled up his hand and slapped me.

The slap resounded.

I touched my face in disbelief. I could feel hot blood where his nails had struck me.

"You disobeyed," he said.

He looked into me.

"Next time you do that," he continued, "it will be a bear's claw that slaps you. I don't know what the bear will look like, but it certainly will be a bear's claw that slaps you."

I feigned happiness as I walked back. I tried not to stomp. It seemed an age before I came back to the house; I climbed up the wall and into my room and sat on my bed, furious. The sounds of jubilation around me did not help.

He came up, and said, "We've been invited to visit someone while people are building a fire."

A man was at the entryway; I followed him, and my hosts, through some streets into a room. There was something odd, it seemed; I could not have thought of this at the time, but while the other people paid no heed to my anger, but all of the people with me subdued their joy. Suddenly we walked in a door, and I saw a beautiful girl, holding a clay tablet and a stylus. The whole world seemed brighter.

Fortress said, "How is our lovely ventriloquist?"

She looked at him as if her face were melting. I looked at Fortress, and he raised his hand slightly. He would tell me the story later.

The man exchanged reverences with me and said, "Welcome, bear slayer. My name is Vessel. My daughter is Silver, and my wife is Shadow. Find a place to sit. Will you have a glass of wine?" His wife unstopped a bottle.

The girl said, "Father Dear, will you tell us a story? You tell us the best stories."

I said, "Please. I miss listening to a good storyteller."

Vessel said, "In another world, there was a big forest on an enormous mountain. There were plants that grew gems as their flowers, only they were so rare it would be easier to take the gems from a mine--and people didn't harvest them, because the plants were so beautiful. It would have been a sacrilege.

"There was a dark stone hut, round as a leaf, and in it a Teacher as old as the mountains, with wisdom deep as its mines. He had a gravelly voice, like a dull and rusty iron dagger slowly scraped across granite. He--"

Silver interrupted. "Bear slayer, some time you must listen to my father sing."

The man continued as if nothing had been said. "The forest was rich and verdant, and every morning it was watered by a soft rain."

At the sound of the word "rain," I suddenly felt homesick. It rained frequently on my island, but here--I had not seen rain at all.

Silver said, "Rain is a natural wonder that happens when a great ball of grey wool, lined with cotton of the purest white, sails in the Abyss and drops packets of water. Apparently this wonder has been seen in this city, though not within the time it would take a mountain to be ground to dust. This did not stop my father from making a tub on the top of our roof, putting sealed pipes down, so that he could pour water from a pipe in our room if Wind were ever silly enough to blow some of that grey wool over this city."

Vessel placed a hand over his daughter's mouth and continued. "He was a many-sided sage, learned in arts and wisdom. Among the things he crafted were a ferret, so lifelike you could believe it was real. If you forcefully squeezed both sides, it would walk along in its own beautiful motion."

Silver pulled her Father's hand down and said, "I think I saw one of those wonders from a travelling street vendor. I looked at some of the craftsmanship and heard some of the gears turning. It must have been made by someone very competent, probably not someone from this city. That didn't stop Father Dear from--"

The man stood up swiftly, flipping his daughter over his shoulder, and walked into the hallway. Shadow said, "That story didn't last long, even for our family. May I serve you some more wine?"

Vessel walked out, holding a key. "Please excuse the disturbance. I have locked Silver in her room. As I was--"

Silver slid through the doorway, stretching like a cat waking from its sleep, and ostentatiously slid two metal tools into a pouch in her sleeve. "I'm disappointed, Father Dear. Normally when we have guests, you at least put something heavy in front of the door."

Some time later, I saw Vessel and Silver sitting together. Pool, Silver, and Shadow had left, and I could hear the warm rhythm of women's talk and laughter from a nearby room. Fortress said, "We were waiting for you. The other hunters have pulled the bear in. Come to the roast!"

I wanted to ask them something, but there were more footfalls outside. I could already hear the drummers beginning to beat out a dance, the singers with their lyres, the priests with their merry blessings, the game players, and the orators with their fascinating lectures. It was not long before we were at the city center.

A young man pulled me off to the side; I saw, on a cloth on the ground, what looked like several pieces of a puzzle. "And now," another man said, "you push the pellet in, and fit the pieces together." He moved his fingers deftly, and I could see what looked like an ordinary crossbow bolt.

"What is that?" I said.

"Let me show you," he said, handing me a cocked crossbow. "Do you see that bag of sand on the roof?"

"Yes."

"Shoot it."

I slowed down, took aim, waited for the target to come to the right place, then fired the crossbow. There was an explosion, and I felt something sting my face. When I realized what was happening, I could feel sand falling in my hair.

I looked at him, confused, and he said, "It's an explosive quarrel. The head contains a strong explosive."

"Why was the shaft made of puzzle pieces? I don't see what that added to the explosion."

He laughed. "The pieces fly out to the sides, instead of straight back at you. It's quite a powerful explosion--you might find it a safer way to kill a bear."

I made a face at him, but I was glowing. So these people knew already that I had killed the bear.

I spoke to one person, then another, then heard people clapping their hearts and calling out, "Speech! We want a speech from the bear-slayer!"

I stood, at a loss for words, then listened for the Wind blowing--but I heard only my name. I listened more, but heard nothing. Then I said, "I am Unspoken," and then the Wind blew through me.

"I am Unspoken," I continued, "and I love to peer into unspoken knowledge and make it known, give it form, or rather make its form concretely visible. Each concrete being, each person, each tree, each divine messenger, is the visible expression of an idea the Light holds in his heart, and which the Light wants to make more real. And his presence operates in us; he is making us more real, more like him, giving us a more concrete form. You know how a creator, making art or tool or book, listens to what a creation wants to see, wrestles with it and at the same time bows low before it, sees how to make it real; that is how the Light shines in us. And when we listen to the Unspoken and give it voice, we are doing what a craftsman does, what the Light does with us. How do we give voice to an unspoken idea, an unspoken expression? We can't completely do so; what we can say is always a small token of what we cannot say. But if the Wind is blowing through us, we may make things more visible." I continued at length, turning over in my spirit the ideas of tacit knowledge and invisible realities, visible, and the divine act of creation reproduced in miniature in us. I traced an outline, then explored one part in great detail, then tied things together. When my words ended, I realised that the Wind had been blowing through me, and I felt a pleasant exhaustion. The festivities continued until we greeted the dawn, and I slept through most of the next day.

All this excitement made my chores in the workshop an almost welcome relief. It began to wear thin, though, after perhaps the third or fourth consecutive day of dismantling tiny devices and then staring at tiny gear teeth to see if they were too worn to use. I began to grow tired of being called 'bear-slayer'--was there nothing else to know about me?--and there was an uneasy silence between Fortress and me about what I had done. He did not mention it; why not? I was afraid to ask.

I worked through each day, and had an hour to my own leisure after the songs at vespers. Mostly I walked around the city, exploring its twists and passageways. It was on one of these visits that I heard a whisper from the shadows, beckoning. It sounded familiar.

"Who is it?" I said.

The voice said, "You know me. Come closer."

I waited for the voice to speak. It, or rather she, was alluring.

I stepped forward, and sensed another body close to my own. A hand rested lightly on my shoulder.

"Meet me here tomorrow. But now, go home."

As I walked home, I realized whose voice it was, and why I didn't recognize it. It was someone memorable, but she had changed somehow, and something made me wary of the change. Yet I wondered. There was something alluring about her, and not just about her.

The following morning, Fortress looked into me and said, "No."

Then he left me in the workshop, and I was torn as I sifted through the day's parts. I was trying to understand my intuitions--or at least that's what I told myself. What I didn't tell myself was that I understood my intuitions better than I wanted to, and I was trying to find some way of making what I understood go away. I touched my cheek, and felt the healing wounds. Then I made up my mind to stay in the building that night.

Evening came, and I realised how long I'd been sitting one place. So I got out, and began walking the other way--just a short distance, to stretch my legs. Then I remembered a beautiful building in the other direction, and I walked and walked. Then I remembered something I had overheard--Fortress's first rebuke had not been everything it seemed. And I found myself in the same place, and felt a soft hand around my wrist. As we walked, and as I could feel my heart beating harder, the ground itself seemed to be more intense. I followed her through twisted passageways, then climbed down several rungs to a place barely lit by candlelight. A strange scent hung around the air. There was something odd, but I could not analyse what. I saw a man in a midnight blue robe bow deeply before me.

"Welcome, Bear Slayer. You did right to kill the bear."

"How did you know--" I began.

"Never mind that. You did the right thing. Fortress is a fine man and a pillar of the community, and we all need him picking apart devices, day after day--or has he asked you to take that task so he can do something interesting? Never mind. Fortress is a fine man, but you are called to something higher. Something deeper."

My heart pounded. I looked. He looked at me with a gesture of profound respect, a respect that--something about that respect was different, but whenever I tried to grasp what the difference was, it slipped out of my fingers.

"Your name is indeed Unspoken, and it is truer than even he knows. You were touching an unspoken truth when you left your pike and attacked the bear."

I couldn't remember any unspoken Wind, or any sense of good, when I disobeyed, and I was excited to learn that what I wanted to remember was true.

"And I have many things to teach you, many lessons. You were not meant to be staring at gear after gear, but--"

It seemed too good to be true, and I asked him, "When will I be able to begin lessons?"

He said, "You misunderstand me. I will teach you. But go back to him; you have learned enough for tonight. My lessons will find you, and show you something far greater than sorting gear after gear, a power that--but I say too much. Go. I will send for you later."

My stomach was tight. I was fascinated, and trying not to realise that something wanted to make me retch. "But please," I said. My voice cracked.

The man shook his head.

I said, "At least tell me your name."

"Why do you ask my name?"

I heard a sound of a blade being drawn, and a crowd parted to reveal a man holding an unsheathed sword. "Clamp! Do not send him out yet!"

The man who had spoken to me drew a dagger, his face burning red. "Poison! How dare you!"

"How dare I? You should not have held the place of glory to begin with. You--"

"Do you challenge me?"

"I do."

What happened next I am not completely sure of. Part of it I could not even see. But what I did see was that Poison was great enough a swordsman to make a mighty swing in a tight room.

I saw him swing.

Then I saw Clamp raise his dagger to parry.

Then I heard a high pitched shattering sound.

Then there was a flurry of motion, and Clamp fell over, dead.

In his hand was a sword hilt, and nothing more.

Clamp turned to me, and said with surprising sweetness, "Do come back, my child. Fortress is a fine man, and no doubt he will teach you many important things. We will see each other later."

I was almost dumbfounded. I stammered, "How did you-- What kind of power lets you--"

He bowed again, very deeply. "Farewell to you. We will meet again."

"Please."

"You need sleep. You have a long day ahead of you."

I stood in place, then slowly walked out. I was elated when I heard his voice call after me, "If you really must know something... Everything you have been told, everything you believe, is wrong. Illusion. You just began to cut through the Illusion when you killed the bear. 'Wisdom is justified by her children.' But don't try to understand the Illusion--it is a slippery thing, profoundly unspoken, and we will see each other soon enough. I'll find you; my classroom is everywhere. Do sleep well. Fortress is a fine man, worthy of respect and worthy to teach you, and I do not doubt he will teach you many exciting and important things."

I walked back, my heart full of recent happenings. I got into bed, and pretended to sleep.

That morning, I felt like my body was made of frosty sludge. I got up, and when Fortress looked at me, I forced myself to bow to him.

That was the last time I bowed to him in a long while, or indeed showed him reverence of any sort. I resented it even then.

I resented the day's sweeping and cleaning, but some of my thoughts congealed. Some of my unspoken thoughts began to take solid form. The respect I had been shown--it was different from the respect I was used to. It meant something different, something fundamentally different. It said, "From one noble soul to another." And the place of meeting was devoid of any adornment, any outer beauty. It had the sense of a place of worship, but as a place it was empty, almost as if it were irrelevant to--there was another thought in the back of my mind, but I could not grasp it.

That night, I thought I heard the sound of Fortress crying. I smiled and slept soundly.

The next morning, Fortress said, "Unspoken, you've seen a lot of gears, but I don't think I've shown you how to make a cam. Cams are terrifically interesting, both in terms of making them and what you can make with them. I'd like to show you how to make cams, then some intriguing devices that use cams. Thank you for the sorting you've done; we should be able to pull exactly the parts we need. Let me heat up the fire, and then we can both work together." He looked at me, and seemed surprised at the boredom in my face. We did exactly what he said, and I made several new types of cam, one of which he really liked. There was wind blowing in my ear, but I couldn't open up and listen to it--I merely wondered that this new activity was even duller than sorting broken parts.

At the end of the day, I said, "When are we going to have a Lesson? I mean a real one?"

He looked at me, held his breath, and said, "I can only think of one Lesson for now. It is not one that you would like."

I said, "Please?"

He said, "Humility is the hinge to joy and the portal to wonder. Humility is looking at other things and appreciating them, instead of trying to lift yourself up by pushing them down. If you push things down, that is the road to misery. Pride pushes things down, and it cuts it off the one thing that could bring joy.

"You are seeking joy where joy is not to be found. Seek it elsewhere, and it will find you."

I hastened out to the street.

Once on the street, I went where I had gone before, but no one reached out to me. I explored, and found several people talking, gardens, statues, and a bookstore I'd not seen before, but there was nothing that interested me. Where was Clamp?

I went back home, and Fortress said, "Have you heard of the Book of Questions?"

I feigned interest. "I've heard about it, and it sounded fascinating," I said, truthfully. "I'd like to hear what you can tell me," I lied.

"I was just thinking about one of the questions, 'What is reverence?'

"There are three things that we do when we reverence each other. We make on ourselves the great sign, and we bow before each other, and we kiss each other.

"The Sign of the Cross is the frame that sets the display of reverence in place. We embrace each other in the Cross's mighty shadow.

"Bowing is the foundation of all civilized discourse. When we bow, we lower ourselves before another; we acknowledge another's greatness. That is the beating heart of politeness; that is the one reason why politeness is immeasurably more than a list of social rules.

"A kiss is everything that a bow is and more. A kiss is a display of reverence, and of love. Do you know why we kiss on the mouth?"

I looked at him, not seeing his point. "What do you mean? Where else would one kiss?"

"I have travelled among the barbarian lands, and there are tribes where a kiss on the mouth is the sort of thing that should be saved for one's wife, or at most one's family." He must have seen the look on my face; he continued, "No, they are not distant from each other, and yes, they live together in genuine community. It is altogether fitting and proper, and our embrace would be out of place in that land. Just because you or I would find it strange to pull back from our brethren this way, as if we were talking to someone through a wall, does not change the fact that it is woven into a beautiful tapestry in their community.

"But let us return to our lands. Kissing on the mouth is significant because it is by our mouth that we drink from the Fountain of Immortality. We reverence the Temple when we enter it, kissing the door and entrance; we ourselves are the Temple, and our mouths are the very door and entrance by which the King of Glory enters when we Commune. Our mouths are honored in a very special way, and it is this very place that we show our reverence.

"But there is another reason. It is by our mouths that we breathe the wind, that we spirit; it is the very spirit that is present in the mouth, and our spirits are knitted together. So the kiss is everything the bow is, and more, and it is the fitting conclusion when we reverence each other. It is communion."

I listened with interest. His words almost pulled me out of my misery.

He closed his eyes, and then said, "Do you know how long it is since you have kissed me?"

I began to approach him.

He pushed me away. "Stop. Go and learn to bow, truly bow. When you have learned to bow, then you may kiss me."

I walked out of the room, pretending to conceal my fury.

Dull, empty day passed after dull, empty day. Fortress tried to teach me things, and I really had no doubts that he was a fine man, but... whatever the great Illusion was, he not only believed it; he couldn't think to question it. I found Silver from time to time, and had comfort by her, but... I didn't understand why she wouldn't take me in to the group. And the rest of the world grew bleaker and bleaker.

Then it happened.

I snuck behind her one day, never giving a hint of my presence, until I found myself led into the chamber, the meeting place. They were chanting; there was something elusive about the chant, and I remained hidden in the shadows. Then Clamp himself saw me in the dark, and said, "Welcome. You have made it." There was a wicked grin on his face.

"Why did you not call me back? Why did Silver not lead me here? Was I not worthy?"

"You were not. Or, I should say, you were not worthy then. We were testing you, to see when you would make your own way in--then you were worthy. That you have come is proof that you are worthy--or at least might be. It does not speak well of you that you took so long. Look at me. Your very face tells me you have been drained by things unworthy of you--dull people, trivial lessons, a warhorse being taught the work of a mule.

"Or at least that's what I could say being generous. I think you are still enmeshed in the Illusion--it is still quite strong in you. So strong that it can probably affect what you see, make what is before your eyes appear to be what it is not.

"There is another test before you. Take this dagger."

He placed in my hand a stone dagger with a serpentine curve to it. It was cold; a coldness seemed to seep through my body and my heart began to pump the icy chaos of a sea at storm. I felt sick.

"There is a clay dummy in the next room, exquisitely fashioned. Place this dagger where its heart would be. You will cut through the illusion, and be ready to drink of the Well of Secrets."

I walked. Aeons passed each footstep; each footfall seemed like a mountain falling and beginning to crumble. And yet it seemed only an instant before I was in the next room.

My stomach tightened. I could not say what, but something was wrong. There was something like a body that was deathly still.

I could see the feet only; the face was covered. Some Wind blew in the recesses of my heart, and I tried to close it out.

I walked over, my stomach tighter. The Wind inside me was blowing louder, leaking, beginning to roar. And then I smelled a familiar smell. How could they make clay smell like--

I twisted the dagger and tore the cloth off the dummy's face. It looked like Fortress. Then Wind tearing through me met with the breath of his nostrils.

I gasped.

I threw up.

There was a sound of laughter around me--or laughing; I could never call it mirth. It was cruel and joyless, and tore into me. And still I retched.

"Do you need help? Or are you really so weak as that?

"Maybe you didn't belong here; not all who merely force their way in are truly worthy."

I looked around on the ground, and saw Fortress's staff.

In a moment I snatched the staff, and cast away the dagger.

I stood, reeling.

"I am not worthy. I am not worthy to be here, still less to be with Fortress. And I'd like to take a heroic last stand, and say that if you're going to kill him--if whatever black poison you've used won't already do so--you'll have to kill me first, but I would be surprised if I could achieve any such thing against you. I cannot call myself Fortress's disciple; that illusion is broken to me. But if I may choose between reigning with you and being slaughtered with Fortress, I can only consider being slaughtered with Fortress an honor that is above my worth and reigning with you to be unspeakable disgrace!"

Clamp looked at me with a sneer. "I don't know why I ever let you in, disciple of Fortress." He grabbed a sword, and made one quick slice.

I felt hot blood trickling down my chest.

"Go on, to your fascinating gears and your deep, deep lessons. Carry your Teacher. We'll meet again. Now I don't think you're worth killing. I don't know what I'll think then."

The blood flowing down my chest, I picked up my unconscious Teacher and his staff.

"The path out is that way. Never mind the drops of blood; you won't reach us this way again."

As I carried his heavy body towards the marketplace and then his home, I panted and sweated. Fortress seemed to be regaining consciousness. I staggered across the threshold and then laid him on the bed.

Pool looked ashen. "Are you all right, Salt?"

Fortress looked at her. "Never mind me; the poison they used is short-lived. I'll simply need more sleep for a few days, and life will go on. Look at Unspoken. I have not been that stunned by a man's behavior in many years."

I collapsed on the floor, then rose to my knees. "Fortress. I have sinned against Heaven and before you. If you have any mercy, show one more mercy that I do not deserve. Give me money that I may return to my island, and no more inquire into things too wonderful for me."

Fortress turned to Pool. "Get one gold sovereign, a needle, and thread."

I looked at him. "One gold sovereign? But that would buy more than--"

"Bite this," he said. "I'll try to make the stitches small."

"I still do not understand," I said.

"Never mind. Tell me what our robes mean."

"Your robe is blue, the color of starry Heaven. Your gift is the one thing needful, to be focused on the Light himself. My robe is green, the color of earth. My gift is to attend to many things on earth. I have wanted to gain the higher--"

"The green robe, and all that it symbolises, is needed, and I do not think you appreciate your gift. And not only because both of us look to the Light and attend to the Creation it illuminates. Place the two colors on the Cross."

"That is a child's exercise."

"Place the two colors on the Cross."

"The blue robe is the color of the vertical arm of the cross, the great tree whose roots delve fathoms down into earth and whose top reaches to Heaven. It is our connection with the Light. The green robe is the color of the cross's horizontal arm, connecting us with other creations. Is there a reason you ask me this?"

He placed his finger at the top of my chest, at the very center--at the top of my wound.

Then he ran his finger down the freshly stitched skin.

I winced in pain.

"It seems you are not a stranger to the blue robe."

My jaw dropped when his words unfolded in my mind. "Fortress, I cannot believe you. Before, you were being generous. Now you are being silly. This wound is not the arm of the cross reaching from Heaven down to earth. I earned this by my own wickedness, and you would destroy me if you knew what evil I had done."

"Are you sure?"

"Fortress, this evil is far worse than lust. It lures you with excitement, then drains the wonder out of every living thing. What are you doing?" I stared in horror as he removed his robe.

"Look at me."

I closed my eyes.

"Trust me."

I opened my eyes, and looked upon his body. Then I looked again. There was a great, ugly, white scar across the top of his chest. He made the sign of the cross on himself, and when his fingers traced out the horizontal arm of the cross, the green arm, I saw his fingers run over the scar.

"I know that pain better than you think."

I was unable to speak.

"Pool is getting you something to eat. You've had quite a difficult time, and your pain will continue. Let's spend tomorrow at the Temple, and then we can get to tinkering."

I was weak, and my wound pained me, but there was a different quality to the pain.

I felt weak. Still, as I entered the Temple, it didn't matter. Once inside the doors, I was in Heaven, and Heaven shone through earth more clearly than it had for long. I smelled the fragrant incense, the incense that ascends before the divine Throne day and night and will ascend for ever.

I walked into the middle part of the Temple, and lay down on the cool, unhewn stone floor, drinking in the glory. I looked through the ceiling at the Heavens: the ceiling was beautiful because it was painted with the blood of sapphires, and more beautiful because it was not sealed. It had chinks and holes, through which the Heaven's light shone, through which the incense continued to rise, and through which Wind blew. I could hear it howl and whisper, and I looked at the Constellations, all seven of which blazed with glory.

I saw the Starburst, a constellation in which one single Glory shot out many rays, and then these many rays coalesced into the one Glory. I let it resonate. I thought of the Creator, from whom all things come and to whom all things return. I thought of learning one thing, then learning many things, then finding the one interconnected whole behind them all.

I looked at the Window of Heaven: a saint shining through a picture. What was it of symbol that was captured so well? In the Constellation one could see the present connection between the saint and the Icon he shone through, indeed itself a window into how the divine Glory shines in a man.

I saw the threefold Tower: on the ground level was body, and then the lower of the upper floors was that which reasons and assembles thinking together, and the higher of the upper level was that which sees in a flash of insight precisely because it is connected, indeed the place one meets the Glory. What were some of the other nuances of these levels?

Then I looked at the Sword, the Great Sword in the War that has been fought since before ever star shone on dew-bejewelled field and will be fought until stars themselves are thrown down, trampled under those who laughed as children among the dew. It sweeps wherever there is Wind, larger than a mountain, smaller than a gem-collecting aphid, stronger than the roaring thunder, so sharp that it sunders bone and marrow. Why, indeed, was it given to men?

The Chalice, the great and Sacred Chalice itself, that held the fluid more precious than ichor, the fount of incorruptibility, a fount that will never be quenched though the mountains should turn to dust and dust turn to mountains. The Chalice from which we drink, the Chalice we kiss when we kiss the--why again should men be so highly exalted?

The Rod and Staff, as ever, were crossed against each other. "Your Rod and Staff comfort me," rise in the chant. The Staff's curves offered comfort to a straying sheep, I knew. And the Rod that went with it--a club with metal spikes, ready to greet predators. A shepherd was a hardened man, an armed guard ready to fight with his life when wolves came to destroy his sheep.

And last, the Steel Orb--a ball, rolling all around an animal hide as the hands at its edge moved up and down, making a slope now here, now there, now a valley, now a shifting plain. The Steel

Orb indeed moved throughout the two levels--or was it really one?--of the threefold Tower, now here, now there, now met by complex construction, now silence, now a flash of inspiration. The Steel Orb is the inner motion that is inseparably connected with the world of invisible truths. It is the ear that listens when the Wind blows. It is the placid pool that reflects all that is around it.

I closed my eyes. Then I looked at the Eighth Constellation, the whole starry roof. The Greatest Feast, when death itself began to move backwards, must have come early that year, about as early as possible; the Constellations stood fixed as they had appeared the year the Temple had begun, just after the day began, and the great Vigil began. There couldn't really be a more representative night to represent the year, nor a better time of that day to stand in.

My breath was still; I stood up, reverenced Fortress and the other Icons, then found the waiting priest and cast off my sins in penitent confession. I do not even remember feeling relieved from that, which is strange: I stood in the stillness as it became song, as voices rose in chant, and the morning was greeted and the divine liturgy began.

I do not remember the liturgy; I do not remember even when the liturgy ended and the priest held a healing service and anointed me with the oil of restoration. What I remember was when it ended, and there were people all around me, their faces alight. It was like waking from a dream, a dream of which one remembers nothing save that there was an inexpressible beauty one cannot remember.

I walked home in Fortress's shadow, and only then remembered something that didn't fit. I remembered--or thought I remembered--the priest's strange advice after my confession: "Be careful. You have a difficult journey ahead of you."

Fortress sat down in front of the work bench. He picked up one gear, then set it down, then rooted through some axles, and sat back.

"Unspoken, I've asked you to sort gears, take machines apart, put machines together, melt gears down, and forge new gears from the molten metal. I've asked you to repair machines, and tell me when gears were made of too soft of a metal. What I haven't asked you to do is tinker. So we'll have a race. Today you can think, and I'll make a mechanical cart. Then you can make a mechanical cart tomorrow. And we'll see, not whose cart can go fastest, but whose cart can go farthest in the smooth part cloister. This will be part ideas and part choosing the best parts. Why don't you go up to your room? You'll have the range of this workshop tomorrow."

I paced up and down my room. I thought. There were several coiled springs in the workshop; having seen some of his previous designs, I was almost sure he would make something spring-powered that would go the distance the spring kept. And how was I to outdo that? He would probably know what spring was best, and he would almost certainly know how to choose parts that moved with each other.

A faint whisper of Wind blew in my mind. I turned over different designs of springs--could I make something more powerful with two springs? The Wind grew, slightly more forceful, and I tried to make it tell me how to best use springs. It became more and more forceful, but I was afraid to drop everything and listen. I began to see, not springs at all, but a burning--

Then I sensed something.

There was something that radiated beauty and fascination. I could not see it. But I sensed it.

"Who are you?" I said.

"I am your Guardian," came the answer. "I was sent to you."

I looked. I still could not see anything, but the beauty is overwhelming.

"What is the idea that is slipping? It has fire, and I hot steam, and--"

"Pay no mind to that. It is nothing."

"How can I build a better spring?"

"Don't. Build a simple, spring-driven cart out of good parts. Then take a knife, and nick the axle on your Teacher's wagon.

That is all. It will bind slightly, and your cart will go further. Or it should."

"But--is that fair?"

"Is that fair? He took the first choice of everything, and you know you lack his year's practice. Come. He wants you to surprise him. He wants you to show ingenuity. This is something he wouldn't expect of you."

I thought I could see colors glowing, shifting, sparkling. Somewhere, in the recesses of my being, it was as if a man jumping up and down and shouting. It was almost enough to draw me away.

"But how can I find his cart? Surely he will hide it, so it will not be a temptation to me."

"Never mind that. I will show you. Just watch me. I was sent here to draw you into Heaven's beauty."

Entranced, I watched the colors shift. It tasted--I tasted the same excitement, the icy brilliance of lightning and the tantalizing heat of lust. I never knew that Heaven could be so much like my former craft.

The next day I built a craft, but no pleasure came from it. It was drained of pleasure, but I was looking for that enticing presence. It seemed to have gone.

Where was Fortress's cart? I couldn't see it. I looked in nooks and crannies. Something seemed wrong. Then... I was aware of the bad intuition first. But I heard a shimmer. "Look right in front of you."

Ahead of me, on top of a pile of disassembled devices, was a cart.

I took a blade, and nicked one of the axles.

The shimmer spoke. "One more thing.

"Look at me."

I looked, and the beauty seemed at once more intense and hollow--and I could not look away.

"Sing an incantation over it."

"What?"

It seemed as if a dark hand was pushing me forward.

I chanted, and watched in horrid fascination. Something seemed to shimmer about my cart. Whenever I looked at it, it seemed the same, but whenever I turned away, it seemed as if there was some beautiful incense rising from it.

The next day, it easily won.

Fortress looked at his cart crossly, with consternation and puzzlement. He seemed to be looking through it.

The next thing I remember was retching, on the workbench. Fortress and a priest were standing over me, although I did not notice them at the time. All I could notice for the time being was an overpowering stench. I wanted to keep retching forever. My spirit was sapped.

"That was not a Guardian," the priest said. "You have listened to a Destroyer."

"If you meet that presence again, make the Sign of the Cross and say, 'Lord, have mercy.'"

I looked at him weakly. "What can I do? I thought I had repented."

"You have repented, and you need to repent again. Pray and fast this week, then make your confession, and come to the Table. Don't go anywhere near that shimmer, no matter how attractive it is. Run, and invoke the Holy Name. And talk with Fortress and me. And if you fall again, repent again. The saints are all praying for you."

I tried to take it in. His words stung me--not because of what he said, but because of why it would be appropriate to say them.

He reverenced me, bowing low. I felt something in his reverence.

With Fortress's leave and the priest's, I went to the monastery to spend my time in prayer and fasting. I took a lump of dry bread each day, and some water.

As the hours and prayers passed, my head seemed to clear. Foul desires raged, but I just resisted them.

The third day after I was at the temple, I ate nothing, and

sang songs, and my body seemed lighter. I remembered the secret learnings I'd made, and they seemed vile, paltry. As the sun set, I suddenly thought of Silver. I was off here, selfishly caring for myself, while she was in the vile grip that squeezed me! I stole out of the monastery, and found her almost immediately.

She placed an arm around my waist. I pulled back, but she held me and said, "I'm just placing an arm around your waist. What is it?" I spoke with urgency and concern, and she 'just'... I do not wish to recall the full shame, but when it was over, Clamp stood over me and threw a hemp belt. "Bind his hands."

As I was walking, captive, I thought of the advice the priest had given me. But how was I to make the sign of the cross? I could try. I tried to move my hands, hoping something miraculous might happen.

Clamp struck my face, and said, "Don't try to wriggle out."

My face stung. I held my tongue, and then let out a rebel yell: "LORD, HAVE MERCY!"

The world seemed to move like melting ice.

Drip.

Drip.

Drip.

I watched every detail of rage flare in Clamp's face.

I heard a shift of cloth and bodies moving.

I saw his hand raised, to strike a crushing blow to my face...

...and descend...

...and caught in the talons of an iron grip.

I did not turn my head. I was too bewildered to look and see why my face was not stinging.

I had somewhere heard that voice before. It seemed familiar. And it was speaking quietly.

I had heard this voice speak quietly in contentment. I had heard it speak quietly to tell a secret. I had heard this voice speaking quietly in banter. What I had not heard was this voice speaking quietly because it was beyond rage, a rage that had gone beyond burning fire to be cold enough to shatter ice.

"Let him go," the voice hissed.

I recognized the voice of my Teacher.

"Let him go," Fortress glared.

Clamp laughed, and let go of me. "Fortress! How wonderful to see you! May I get you a glass of wine?"

Fortress began working on my bands. He said nothing.

Clamp said, "A great Teacher like you has much to offer, could probe much secret wisdom. You seemed to have a knack for--"

I felt my stomach quiver.

A crowd was beginning to form around us: no one was right by us, but many were looking.

Fortress said, "No."

My stomach knotted. I had an overwhelming sense that I should move.

I obeyed it.

Clamp looked at Fortress.

Fortress looked at Clamp.

The anger in Fortress's face began to vanish.

Clamp seemed to be leaving fear and entering terror.

I backed off further.

I saw a faint ripple of muscles across Clamp's body.

I began to scream.

Metal sang as a sword jumped from its sheath.

I saw, moment after horrid moment, the greatsword swing into the side of Fortress's head.

Then I heard a shattering sound, and when I realised what was happening, Clamp had been thrown up against the far wall, while Fortress was in the same place.

The sherds of a sword hilt dropped from Clamp's hand.

The anger vanished from Fortress's face. He looked, and said, "Come back, Clamp. We need you."

I could hear the sadness in his voice.

Clamp ran away in abject terror.

I had been fasting. Even if I had not been fasting, I would have...

I fainted.

My head slowly began to clear--much more slowly because Fortress was carrying me again.

"I'll sleep at your doorway at the monastery," Fortress said, "and fast with you."

I closed my eyes. "I'm sorry. I don't deserve to--"

"Not as punishment, Unspoken. You've endured punishment enough; harsh fasting and vigils are a much lighter load than--but you are weak and vulnerable now. You need the support. And I would like to share this with you."

The fasting passed quickly. Or more properly, it moved very slowly, and it was hard, but there was cleansing pain. The Wind moved through me, and gave me respite from my burdensome toil of evil.

When it was the eighth day, Fortress and I returned to the Temple. A mighty wind was blowing all around, and its song and its breath moved inside. Wind blew through every jewel of the liturgy. And there was--I couldn't say.

After the end of the liturgy, when I was anointed for healing, Fortress said, "Let's go home and get to work. Pool has some money to buy a chicken, and--why are you hesitating?"

"Could I return to the monastery and fast for another week?"

"Why? You have done what the priest asked. You needn't do more. There is no need to engage in warfare above your strength. Remember, the Destroyers always fast."

"That's not why."

"Why, then?"

"That's what I am trying to find out."

I prayed and fasted, and my head seemed to clear. I succeeded that week from returning to my vomit; I think it was because Fortress spent the week with me, and he was generous to spend that long without seeing Pool. He prayed with me, and at the end, my mind took on a new keenness. I still did not know what it was the Wind was trying to tell me.

But I no longer resisted it. Fortress gently said, "You have fasted further, and I will trust you that it was the right thing to do.

But why not let this fast meet its summit in a feast? I can buy a chicken, and we can sit down at table."

"But the--"

"Do not worry about that. If the Wind holds a message for you, the Wind will make that clear enough. Let's return."

Once home, I asked him a simple question. I think the question was, "Why are you so concerned for me?" Or it might have been, "What is your experience with the poison I tasted?" Or something else. And he gave a long and interesting answer to me.

I don't remember a word he said.

My stomach was full of roast chicken, dried lemon, and all the bread I wanted. Pool was generous with wine. Fortress's voice was humming with the answer to whatever question I asked, and I could hear the chatter and laughter of small children in the background. It concentrated my thoughts tremendously.

What was your error?, the Wind whistled in my ear.

In a moment, I searched through the evils I committed and drew in a breath. Pride, I said in my heart. The primeval poison that turned the Light-Bearer into the Great Dragon. The one evil that is beyond petty sins like lust.

You embraced that evil, but what was your error?

I drew in another breadth. Everything. Lust. Magic. Scorning the beauty of the Light. Seeking to order the world around myself. As I think over the great evils that exist, I do not see that I am innocent of any one of them, nor free of their disease.

Those wrongs have been obliterated forever. They are no more. You are innocent of them. You are being healed. The vilest of these, your pride itself, is a smouldering coal thrown into the infinite Ocean. What was your error?

I do not understand. I have hardly made errors greater than these--if 'error' is even the word. Do you mean something small by 'error'?

No, something great and terrible. What was your error?

I do not understand.

What was your error?

With my inner eye, I saw the pelt and the Steel Orb, only frozen. The Steel Orb needed to move, but it was locked in place. Those words haunted me, chased me, yelled at me. I long lie awake that night, searching to see what was being asked. At last, as the pale light of the dawn began its approach, I drifted into sleep.

I saw, in vivid detail, the moments of my descent. Only it was different in my dream. When I had actually lived it, I saw things through a veil, through an Illusion. I suffered empty pain, and thought I was gaining wholeness. Now the illusion was stripped away, and I saw every moment how I had thrown away gold to fill my hands with excrement. And every time, the Glorious Man looked at me and asked what the Wind had asked, "What was your error?"

I saw a time when I listened eagerly. I was being told secrets, hidden truths beyond the ken of the ordinary faithful. I was, I had thought, being drawn into the uppermost room and tasting with delight its forbidden fruit. The Glorious Man looked into me, looked through me, and asked, "What was your error?"

I was awake, bolt upright in my bed. My body was rigid. In the window I saw that the dawn had almost come. "Fortress!" I called.

In an instant, Fortress was by my side. "What is it?"

"You have felt the pain I felt."

"Every evil by which you have poisoned yourself, I have done, and worse."

"What was your error?"

He paused a moment, and said, "Pride."

"No. What was your error?"

"More evil than I can remember."

"When you descended into that living Hell, did you embrace evil alone, or did you embrace evil and error?"

He drew in a breath. "Climb up to the roof with me."

The dawn was breaking; stream after stream of golden, many-hued light poured over the edge of the city. We both sat in silence.

Fortress seemed completely relaxed.

I was not.

"Fortress, I did not win our race."

Fortress's eyes greeted the sun.

"I know."

He drank in more of the light, and said, "Would you like to have another race?"

Time passed.

"You can choose who makes his wagon first."

"You make your wagon first."

I drew a breath.

"It must be painful for a Teacher to watch his pupil descend into filth and have to rescue him and carry him back."

"To me, that is a very good day."

I looked at his face, trying to find sarcasm or irony.

I found none.

"Why?"

"Clamp was my pupil."

I didn't know what to say. I fumbled for words. I tried to meet his pain.

"You seem very happy for a man with no children."

I saw tears welling up in his eyes.

I began to stammer.

He said, "Let's go and build our cars. If you want, you can take the silt board so you can design your wagon while I'm building mine. A fair match would be balm to my soul."

I looked at the board. Something was ticking in the back of my mind--fire on the spring, was it? But why? I set to work on the board, trying to reconcile something burning with a spring and gear box. Something was knocking in the back of my mind, but I couldn't listen to it. In the end I told myself I'd make a spring driven wagon with a lamp on top: a large one, that would burn brightly.

The next day, I set about smithing the lamp. I enjoyed it, and it was a thing of beauty. Almost at the end of the day my eye fell on something, and I saw that Fortress had left the best spring for me.

The next day we raced, and I lit my lamp. It burned brightly. It finished two laps, while Fortress's cart made fully twenty laps round the cloister, but he liked the lamp; its flame was a point of beauty. "Keep trying," he said, "although I'm not going to ask why you put a lamp on. I'll be in the workshop sorting gears; could you care for customers?"

At the evening meal Fortress seemed preoccupied; it looked as if he was listening.

We sat in silence.

He moved, as with a jolt. "Unspoken, what were you saying to me when we greeted the coming of the dawn?"

My face turned red.

"No, sorry. I mean, before then."

"I don't know. My sense was that it was something important, but I doubt if--"

Fortress dropped his bread and moved to give Pool a deep kiss. "Come with me, Unspoken."

As we walked, he turned to me and said, "The Great Fast is approaching, and we all need to purify ourselves. You especially."

"But I am working on--"

"That is why you especially need to be purified. Forget that completely."

I recognized the route to the monastery.

"There are some things I can give you, but you need to be at the monastery. As much as you are able, submit discipline as if you were a monk. Draw on their strength. Afflict yourself. Gaze on the glory of the Light."

"But--"

"Trust me."

Not long after, we arrived at the monastery. He spoke briefly with the head monk, Father Mirror, and reverenced me. "The Mother who held the Glory in her arms now holds you in her heart and in her prayers." Then he left.

The rhythm of the calendar, of the week, of the day, became clearer. My head itself became clearer. With the discipline I became hazier and the Glory became clearer.

I was praying in my cell, and suddenly it was illuminated with beauty and light, so that the flame of my lamp could not be seen. I was dazzled, and at the same time uneasy.

I looked, and I saw the form of the Glorious Man. He looked at me and said, "You have done well."

I felt as if there was something jumping up and down, shouting for attention, inside me.

"I will tell you what you are to write about your error."

I was fascinated. Or almost fascinated. I turned my ear to the man jumping up and down. And wrenched myself away.

I bowed my head, and said, "Glorious One, I am not worthy."

Immediately I reeled. A stench, that felt as if I was touching fetid--I do not want to say what it smelled like. I fell backwards, reeling and gasping for breath.

I heard a shuffle of cloth, and then footprints. The chief monk stepped in. He looked displeased, although I wasn't sure he was displeased at me. He bid the other monks leave, and said to me, "My son, tell me everything."

I hesitated. "You need to sleep so you can greet the morning in chant."

"My son, another of my brother monks can lead that greeting even if you are still talking when it comes."

I opened my mouth, and talked, and talked, and talked. He seemed surprised at times, but looked on me with kindness. At the end he said, "I will take the cell next to you and pray with you. The whole monastery will pray over you."

"I am not worthy--"

"And I am not worthy to serve you and give you what strength I can. If it were a question of being worthy--" he shuddered. "Sleep, and rise for the morning chant if you can."

That night I was riven by my dreams.

Evils in me that I thought were dead rose up with new life. I interrupted Father Mirror often, and he told me to pray, "Heavenly Glory, if you want me to fight these impulses, that I will do." And I did. Gradually the fight became easier. I began to count the days, and contemplate the Glory.

As time passed, I lived to join the monks, the stars and the rocks, beings of light, in contemplation above everything else. I looked into the Glorious Light when--

I felt a hand shaking me. I opened my eyes, and collected my presence. Then I closed my eyes and looked away.

"What is it?"

His face was radiant. "I was looking on the Glorious Light, and--"

Silence.

"I am not worthy to look on you. That light is shining through your face. Leave me alone."

"My brother."

I said nothing.

"Look at me."

I turned to face him, keeping my eyes down.

"You would not see this light coming from my face unless it were coming from your face as well."

"You mock me. My face? I am not a monk, nor have I gone through years of discipline. And I have--"

"The Wind blows where it will. You could not see this light at all unless your face were radiant."

I said nothing.

"I have come to call you. It is time for the Great Vigil."

"Time for the Great Vigil? The Great Feast tonight? But it is scarcely a day that has passed since--"

"I know. I am not ready either. But the Feast is here. And those prepared and unprepared are alike compelled by the joy."

I went through the Great Vigil at the monastery, reverenced each of the monks. Then Father Mirror accompanied me home, the dark streets lit by the brilliance of his face. I joined Fortress and Pool in the revelry; I danced with Pool. Then Fortress walked home, one arm over Pool's shoulder and one arm around mine.

When we stepped across the threshold, Fortress said, "It is time for a race."

I let Fortress build his wagon first, and insisted that he take the best spring. Then I sat down with the silt tablet.

My intuition had been to mix fire and water. Or something like that. Or burn water. Or--I sketched one design after another, trying to see how they would help a spring, or gears for that matter. Towards the end of the day, I sat down, perplexed, and wiped the slate clean. I had given up.

That night, I prayed my giving up. Then--it took me a long time to get to sleep.

In the morning, I left the springs alone entirely. I pulled out the metal lamp and made a nearly-sealed water tank to go above it. I put the water tank above the flame, and fitted something special to its mouth. By the end of the day, I was exhausted, and my fingers were sore.

The next day, Fortress wound the spring, and I took a tinderbox and lit the flame. He looked at me slightly oddly, and when he turned his cart around at the end of the first lap, looked at me gently.

My cart hadn't moved.

At the end of the second lap, he asked me, "Did your cart move?"

I said nothing.

At the end of the fourth map, he said, "Your cart is moving."

And it was. Steam from the heated tank was moving one part, which turned gears, to the effect that it was moving very slowly. And it continued moving slowly for the rest of the day, finally stopping after it had run a full seventy-two laps.

Fortress walked away from me with a look of amazement. "Unspoken, I've got to tell my friends about you."

As I was drifting off to sleep, the Wind whistled in my ear: What was your error?

The Steel Orb broke free from one spot, and began to roll,

first one way, then another. It seemed to be exploring its strength, moving just a little this way, just a little that way.

I wrestled in my thoughts, like a man trying to lift a greased boulder. I was not trying to lift it yet; my fingers slid over the surface, seeking purchase.

Thoughts flowed through my mind, wordless thoughts that slid away whenever I tried to capture them in worded form. I grasped after them with patient, eager expectation.

I did not notice when I descended into the depths of slumber.

I was staring into a dark, deep, colorless, shapeless pool, and trying to see its color and shape. There was light behind me, but for the longest time I did not look into it. Then I looked into the light, and turned, and--

A voice said, "Awaken!" and I was shaken awake.

Fortress and Father Mirror were both crouching over me. I sat up, nervously.

"What is it?" I said, flinching against a rebuke.

"Last night, I was speaking with the bishop," Father Mirror said, "when a messenger arrived, limping. He had been severely delayed. A Holy Council has been summoned, and the bishop requests that Fortress, you, and I join him on his travels."

"Me? I would just be a burden."

"Never mind that. He did not tell me his reasons, but he specifically requested that you join him immediately."

"What about--"

"No 'what about'. Will you obey?"

I turned to Fortress. "May I use your crossbow?"

"A crossbow has been packed on your horse."

"On the way out, may I visit a friend?"

"Quickly."

Still in a daze, I reverenced Pool and bade her farewell. Then Fortress gave his farewell, and we found the horses.

I knocked on a door--I thought it was the right door--and said, "I've been summoned on a journey by the bishop, and I do not understand why. But may I buy all of your explosive quarrels?

I have some money I could offer."

"Bear slayer, you may have them. Without money. Just let me get them." He stepped in, and seemed to be taking a long time. I heard more and more rummaging, and Father Mirror sounded impatient. Then he came out, looking sheepish. "I'm sorry. I can't find them. I've looked all around. I wish I--"

"Don't worry about it," I said. "Just remember me."

Before the sun was above the mountains, we were on the Road.

We rode along at a cantor. The horses were sleek and strong, and I placed myself opposite the bishop.

He placed himself next to me.

"My son, I offer my apologies, but I wish to talk with you."

"Why?"

"Tell me about what you did wrong. And what you've done since."

I told him, and he said, "There is something more. What more is there?"

"I don't know how to say. It's just that... something about it seems different from struggling with sin. Like there's something different involved, that is error."

"All sin is error. Pride especially is illusion."

"But... Would you say we believe the same things? Perhaps you understand them better than I, but would you say we believe the same things?"

"Yes, certainly. But they do not believe the same thing. It is not a single mistaken belief."

"What would you say if I said it wasn't just an error in the specific thing one believes, but an error so deep that... an error whose wake said, 'What you believe is private?'"

The bishop turned towards me.

His eyes narrowed.

"The highest part of the inner person is mind, but it is not private. In an immeasurably greater way than the five senses, it connects with and wrestles with and apprehends and conquers and contemplates the spiritual realities themselves. Those who choose error grapple with these realities in the wrong way like--like a man trying to climb a mountain upside down. The mountain is there, and the hands and feet are there, but they're not connected the right way."

The bishop was silent.

"But... When I stepped into that vortex, I had something of a sense that I was breaking away from the mountain, like it was an illusion, and creating my own private hill, and forging the limbs of my body that I could use to connect with it. I--"

The bishop remained silent.

I fumbled. A flash of insight struck. "I was stepping into a secret, hidden reality, rejecting ordinary people's reality. That is pride. But normally when we say 'pride', we mean an evil of which one part is illusion. Here there it is more like the Illusion is the spiritual reality, and bitter pride is its handmaiden. No; that's not quite right. The relationship is--"

He looked at me. "That's enough for now. Let us chant psalms together. I want to hear more, but please, my son, don't believe I'm only concerned with getting that out of you." He paused a moment, long enough for me to realize how tense my body was. "Now Fortress told me you're quite a tinker?"

"He glared," the bishop said, "and said, 'and I will not speak with anyone lower than a bishop!'"

"What did you say," I asked.

"I looked at him wearily, and said, 'Believe and trust me, good man, when I say that no one here is lower than a bishop."

He paused a moment and continued, "Unspoken--"

A flood of memories came back. It was not what he said, but how he said it. He had spoken in my island's dialect. His accent was flawless.

"How do you know my island's dialect?" I asked. "I come from an insignificant and faroff island. Nothing important has ever come from that island, and nothing ever will."

"That's easy enough," he said, "I was born there.

"Unspoken, I am a man like you." He paused, and continued, "There is a place I was born. I have a father and mother, and brothers and sisters. I remember the first time I skipped a stone, the thrill when I reinvented the pipe organ. I contemplate and pray, hunger and--"

"Your Grace, how did your father introduce you to the art of memory?"

"When I was a boy, I loved to swim. I swam as much as I was allowed, and some that I wasn't. There was a lagoon, with a network of underwater caves, and some of them I was allowed to explore. My uncle chipped and ground a mica disc enclosed in a ring of copper, and showed me how to close my eye around it. I could see under the water, and I watched the play of light inside the one largest cave. My uncle also gave me a bent spear, with the head pointing sideways, and I speared many meals with it.

"One day my father looked at me and said, 'Fire, if you could decorate the cavern in the big pool, what would you put there?

"I thought and said, 'Blankets along the wall so I could feel something soft.'

"He said, 'What else?'

"I said, 'Nothing else.'

"'What might you imagine?'

"'There's nothing else that would work.'

"'And things that wouldn't work?'

"I hesitated, and said, 'A candle to see by, and something to write with.'

"'What else?'

"'Come. You are wilder than that.'

"'Color, as when the leaves of the forest go green.'

"'And what if there were passageways branching off? What would you like to see there?'

"He led me to imagine this vast network of rooms and passageways, each one different, each one holding something different, each one different to be in. It was a wonderful game, and swimming was almost as enjoyable as this activity.

"One day, my father added another dimension. He walked up to me with a rope and said, 'Do you see this rope?'

"'Yes,' I said.

"'What is the strangest thing that could happen to it in the antechamber to your labyrinth?'

"'If it were not soaked, for it to fall down to the floor.'

"My father was silent.

"'Or it would be peculiar for it to fall, not up or down, but to the side.'

"I expected a smile. My father looked and me and said, 'Surely you have imagined things stranger than that.'

"I said, 'It could coil and uncoil, slithering around the walls before coming together to a bundle--and then coming together and vanishing.'

"My father smiled and said, 'And what of that plate there? What could happen to it in the room under?'

"I laughed at the things I imagined; such strange things happened to the things in my rooms, and I invented things on my own. Then I began to be bored, and my father saw my boredom. 'This game bores you. Let's move on to something else.

"'Look up. Note what position the stars are in. After ten nights' span, I will open the cover of a box and you will behold forty things you've not seen before. Then I will leave you with the box and eat a large loaf of bread. When I have returned, I will return and we will climb that peak, and when we reach the top, you will tell me everything you saw in the box.'

"I jumped slightly, and waited for him to explain himself.

"When no explanation came, I said, 'I can't carry a wax tablet when I'm climbing the peak.'

"He said, 'Nor would I allow it if you could.'

"I said, 'Then how will I do it?'

"He said, 'I've already told you.'

"I was angry. Never had he been so irrational as this. For seven days I searched my heart in wrath, searching. On the eighth day I rested from my wrath and said, 'He will say what he will say. I renounce anger at his request.'

"He had begun his odd request by releasing me from my labyrinth; I delved into it. I imagined the first room, but I couldn't banish the rope coiling and uncoiling. I swam to another room, only to have something else greet me. I swam around, frustrated again and again when--

"My face filled with shame.

"I spent the next two days playing, resting, swimming. I moved through the imaginary labyrinth. When my father pulled the cover off the box, I placed everything in my imaginary labyrinth, one in each room, exactly as he had taught me. It took him a while to eat the bread, so I stared at the box's rough leather lining. We walked, and talked, and the conversation was... different. I enjoyed it.

"He asked me, 'What was in the box?'

"I said, 'A key, a stylus, a pebble, a glazed bead, a potsherd, a gear, an axle, a knife, a pouch, a circle cord, some strange weed, a stone glistening smooth by the river's soft hands, a statuette, a crystalline phial, a coil of leather cord, a card, a chisel, a mirror, a pinch of silt, a candle, a firecord, a badly broken forceps, a saltball, a leaf of thyme, an iron coin, some lead dregs, a bite of cured fish, a small loaf of spiced bread, some sponge of wine, a needle, a many-colored strand of parchment, an engraved pendant--hmm, I'm having trouble remembering this one--a piece of tin wire, a copper sheet, a pumice, a razor, a wooden shim, a pliers, and a measuring ribbon.'

"'I count thirty-nine,' he said. 'Where's the fortieth?'

"I ran through my rooms and hesitated. 'I memorized thirty-nine things, then stared at the rough leather inside the box. I didn't see another; I don't even have the trace of memory like when there's another one that I can't quite spring and catch.'

"When I said, 'rough leather inside the box,' he seemed pleasantly surprised. I didn't catch it at the time, but I understood later.

"And that was how my father let me taste the art of memory. How did your father teach you the art of memory?"

"I don't have as good a story to tell. He introduced me to the more abstract side--searching for isomorphisms, making multiple connections, encapsulating subtle things in a crystalline symbol."

"Oh, so you've worked with the abstract side from a young age. Then I have something to ask of you."

"Yes?"

"I want to speak with you further. I'd like if you could inscribe in your heart the things you tell me. When we return--pardon, if we return, if we are shown mercy--I may send you to the monastery and ask you to transcribe it so it can be copied."

My heart jumped.

His Grace Fire asked me, "If you were to crystallize your dark journey in one act you did, what would it be?"

I slid my mind through my sins. I watched with a strange mixture of loathing, shame, and haunting desire as I--

"Stop," he said. "I shouldn't have asked that. I tempted you."

I looked at him and blinked. "None of the actions I did encapsulates the journey."

He cocked one eyebrow.

"Or rather, all of them did, but the entire dark path is captured by one action he didn't do. I neither gave nor received reverence."

"That doesn't seem surprising," he nodded. "Pride is--"

"That's also true," I said.

He looked at me.

"In our reverence, we greet one another with a holy kiss. That is hard to appreciate until you have tried to step outside of it. We try to be spiritual people, but however hard we try, matter is always included. Every one of the Mysteries includes matter. We worship with our bodies. Fasting does us good because we are creatures of body--all of the Destroyers fast, all of the time, and never does any of them profit by it. Our great hope is that we will be raised in transformed, glorified and indestructible bodies to gaze on the Light bodily for ever.

"More to the point, the holy kiss is the one act in the entire Sacred Scriptures that is ever called holy."

He blinked. "I hadn't thought about it that way, but you are right."

"And... there was licentiousness; we could do wrong with our bodies, but this is only for the reason that the holy kiss was not possible. The spiritual embrace draws and works through body, because body is part of spirit. Their asceticism and libertinism alike exist because of a wedge between spirit and body."

"How can they do that? That is like driving a wedge between fire and heat."

"Of course you can't," I said, "but they think they can."

"My son," he said, "you are placing things upside down. We fast to subdue our bodies, which have become unruly; spirit and matter are not equal partners, nor is matter the center of things. In this world or the next."

"You're wrong," I said. "You only say that because your approach to spirit has always assumed matter. If you had genuinely lived the life and practice of believing that matter was evil, was not our true selves, not illusion, you would understand and not say that."

I winced when I realized what he'd just said. I waited for his rebuke. Or a slap.

"Go on," he said. "I'm listening."

"Or maybe that was too bold. Spirit is supreme; the Glory is spirit, and those who worship him must worship him in spirit and in truth. But... struggling to subdue matter, and impregnate it with spirit, does not let you realize what place matter has. Returning from despairing in matter as evil is very different."

"Despair?"

"Despair..." I thought. "Matter is evil, probably the evil creation of an evil god. If that is true, you cannot relate to the cosmos with joy, not even abstemenious joy. You must despair in it. And--I think this is connected, it's all connected--if the entire cosmos is an illusion which we must escape, then no less is its creator the same sort of thing. There's a perverse acknowledgment, I think, that the cosmos must reflect its Creator and radiate its glory. Because if they believe this horrible thing about the cosmos, they believe the same about its Creator, and as they transgress the cosmos as an obstacle they get past, so they transgress its Creator as an obstacle to get past. From what I've heard, their pictures of subordinate gods vary, but one of the few common features is that since this cosmos is evil or illusory, and this cosmos must reflect its Creator, the Creator himself must be something we need to get past if we are to find real good."

"You are describing an error that is really more than one error."

"Yes. Things are... private. They consider themselves more spiritual, more of the spiritual power we use to touch spiritual realities, yet somehow they have a hydra's different pictures of what those spiritual realities themselves. In some of them it almost sounds as if that spiritual apprehension is private."

"I won't ask you to inventory everything that was private. Did you see any of the Scriptures?"

"Not many. And those I read were... odd."

"Odd?"

"The Gospels are wondrous documents indeed."

"Indeed."

"But they never pander. Never does a writer say, 'I tell these things that you may be titillated.' However amazing or miraculous the events are, the miracles are always secondary, signs that bear witness to a greater good.

"And I appreciated this after the few occasions I was able to read their Gospels. Those books do not tell the story of when Heaven and Earth met; the ones I read don't tell a story at all; they are collections of vignettes or stories, that suck you in with the appearance of hidden wisdom. They appeal to someone despairing of this cosmos and seeking what is hidden behind it. Your Grace, only when I had tried to dive into those crystallized vortices had I realized how pedestrian the Gospels are: the Glorious Man shines with the uncreated Light and we blandly read that his clothes are white as no fuller on earth could reach them."

"Hmm," he said. "That's like--a bit like the difference between marriage and prostitution. In many ways."

"And... if you understand this basic despair, a despair that forges the entire shape of their relationship to Creation and Creator, you will understand not only their excessive asceticism and their license, their belief that the Light is not good, but also their magic. The incantations and scrolls are in one sense the outermost layer of a belief: if this Creation is evil and illusion, if one must transgress it to find truth, then of course one does not interact with it by eating and drinking, ploughing and sewing. One must interact in hidden, occult ways, and gain powers."

"I see. But don't get into that; I'd rather not have you remember that poison. And I assume you could say much more, but I'm beginning to get the picture, and I want to pray and contemplate the Glory before meeting any more of it.

"How would you summarize it, in a word?

"There are many ways our Scriptures can be summarized in a word: 'Love the Glory with all of your inmost being and your soul and your might, and love your neighbor as yourself.' 'He has shown you, O man, what is good, and what does the Glory require of you, but to do justice, and love mercy, and walk humbly in the Light.' 'The Glory became a Man and the Glorious Man that men might become Glorious Men and Glories.' And this error could be summarized in many ways...

"'Your spirit too pure for this unworthy cosmos.'"

"Take a rest," he said. "I think you've said enough for now. Let's pray."

"Oh, and one other thing. When your heart is set on pushing past the One Glory, there seem to many gods offering their protection and guidance."

"Pray, child. You've said enough."

We reached another city, and Fortress said, "We have a decision to make. The city we want to reach is due East. The road turns, and heads almost directly south."

I said, "Why?"

"Because East of the city is the dark forest."

The bishop looked at him. "I think we can enter the city and buy a good meal. But we lack the time to take the Southern route."

Less than two hours later, we were re-supplied and heading East. It was weeks before we met anything worse than stepping in poison ivy.

At night, I was awoken by the sound of a foot shuffling. I looked around; it was still Fortress's watch, and Bishop Fire and Father Mirror were already getting up. The campfire was burning low, and in the flickering torchlight I saw a ring of many eyes.

"Black wolves," Fortress whispered. "Stand up and mount your horse slowly."

I reached across my bedroll. Fortress hissed, "No. We can't afford that. I don't know what--"

I slid up on my horse and slowly reached for my crossbow. Fortress hissed, "Are you crazy? There are more wolves than quarrels, and they'd be on us by your third shot." Then he cocked his head and said, "Whisper soothing in your horse's ear. And be ready to gallop."

The wolves had become visibly closer in this scant time; one started to run towards Fortress's horse. Then Fortress reared and parted his lips, and bellowed.

I have never heard a man roar that loudly. Not before, not after. It hurts my ears to think about it. He roared like thunder, like waterfall, like an explosion. The wolf was stunned, and immediately he was galloping forward, the wolves running from him in abject terror. It was all I could do to control my horse, and it took some tracking before Fortress found Father Mirror.

We sat in our saddles; every sound, every smell, seemed crisper. Then I realized that tendrils of dawn were reaching around, and as we rode on, we descended into a clearing and His Grace said, "Look! The great city itself: Peace."

It seemed but an hour and we were inside the great city itself. Having taken time to drink our fill of water, but not eat, we came into the great chamber where the holy bishops and the other attendees were gathered.

I could hear Wind blowing. I tried to listen.

"And I know," an archbishop said, "that not everyone can

scale the hidden peaks. But you misunderstand us gravely if you think we are doing a poorer job of what you do."

Several heads had turned when we entered. An archbishop said, "Your Grace Fire! May the Glory grant you many years. Have you any thoughts?"

The Wind whispered in my ear, and quite suddenly I climbed on top of a table in an empty part of the chamber. I ignored the shock of those around me, so intently was I listening to the Wind's whisper.

"If that is anything," I shouted, "but a lie from Outer Darkness, may the Glory strike me down!"

I heard a click, and then several things happened at once. I was thrown violently forward, and I heard an explosion. I felt an unfamiliar sensation in my back, and I tasted blood.

A deathly silence filled the room. I began to move, and slowly picked myself up. "I repeat," I said. "If that is anything but a lie from Outer Darkness, may the Glory strike me down."

There was another explosion, and I felt fire on my back. I stood unmoved.

"I repeat. If that is anything but a lie from Outer Darkness, may the Glory strike me down!"

The Wind whispered, "Duck!"

I ducked, and a crossbow quarrel lodged itself in the wall.

Time oozed forward.

There was a scuffle, and four soldiers entered. One of them was holding a crossbow. Three of them were holding Clamp.

"Fathers and brothers, most reverend bishops and priests, deacons and subdeacons, readers and singers, monks and ascetics, and fellow members of the faithful, may the Glory reside in Heaven forever! I speak from painful awareness that what that son of darkness says is false. That is how it presents itself: a deeper awareness, a higher truth.

"This Council was summoned because you know that there is a problem. There are sins that have been spreading, and when you encourage people to penitence, something doesn't work. It is as if the disease of sin separated us from our natural union with the Light, and when the chasm was deep, the Glorious Man became Man, the Great Bridge that could restore the union... and something strange happened. Men are sliding off the Bridge.

"Fathers and brothers, the problem we are dealing with is not only a chasm that needs to be bridged. The problem is a false path that leads people to slip into the chasm.

"This error is formless; to capture it in words is to behead the great Hydra. It will never be understood until it is understood as error, as deadly as believing that poison is food.

"It is tied to pride; far from enjoying Creation, visible and invisible, however ascetically, it scorns that which we share, and the path of salvation open to mere commoners. It's the most seductive path to despair I've seen. I know. I've been there. The teaching that we are spirit and not body, that there is a sharp cleavage between spirit and body... I don't know how to distinguish this from proper asceticism, but it's very different. When we fast, it is always a fast from a good, which we acknowledge as good when we give it back to the Light from whom every good and perfect gift shines. This is a scorn that rejects evil; I don't know all the mythologies, but they do not see the world as the shining of the Light. The true Light himself would never stain his hands with it; it is the evil creation of a lesser god.

"And it is despair. It tingles, it titillates, it excites at first, and all this is whitewash to cover over the face of despair. Everything that common men delight in is empty to them, illusory joy. The great Chalice, that holds the meat of the Glorious Man's own flesh and holds the fluid more precious than ichor, his own true blood, the fluid that is the divine life--that all who partake see what they believe and become what they behold, younger brothers to the Glorious Man, sons of Light, sustained by the food of incorruption, servants in the Eternal Mansion who are living now the wonder we all await--I will not say what exciting thing they propose to replace it by. Some manage, I know not how, to find greater wonder in saying the Man was not the Glory and the Chalice as we know it is nothing. But it is in the beginning as sweet as honey, and in the end as bitter as gall and as sharp as a double-edged sword. In a word, it says, 'Your spirit is too pure for this unworthy cosmos.'

"It is not healthy to dwell long on such things; I will not tell how its broken asceticism turns to people believing they can do whatever they wish with their bodies. (If the body is evil, not our true self...) He who long gazes into darkness may find his eyes darkened very soon or very slowly. In either case it is not good. But I will say this: Gaze on the Light, be strengthened by the Glorious Man, and listen to the Wind, and the better you know it, the less Darkness will look like Light. And we can rise against this error as error."

The archbishop who spoke when I entered said, "Would His Grace Fire please speak? I believe he has been rudely interrupted."

His Grace Fire looked at him levelly. "I have already spoken," he said, "and I have nothing further to say."

Then His Grace turned to me. "Unspoken. Your robe is damaged beyond repair. Would you like a green or blue robe to replace it?"

My voice quivered. "A green robe was chosen for me. I need to--"

"That isn't what I asked of you. Would you like a green or blue robe to replace it?"

I looked at Fortress.

He fell on his face prostrate before me and said, "Dear Unspoken, you have surpassed my humble tutelage for ever. I release you."

I turned back to His Grace Fire. "A blue robe."

Then I turned to Father Mirror. "To gaze on the glory as a member of your monastery."

A flask of oil was in the bishop's hands. "Unspoken, I give you a new name. You have spoken the unspoken. You have delved into the unspoken, searched it out, drawn forth jewels. I anoint you Miner."

All was still as he anointed my forehead, my eyes, my

mouth, the powers of my body.

The Council's decision was swift. My words had opened a door; insight congealed in the hearts of those present. It moved forward from discussion to decrees, and decrees in turn gave way to the divine liturgy.

I had never been at a Meal like that, and have never been at one since. The uncreated Light shone through every face. I saw a thousand lesser copies of the Glorious Man. The Wind blew and blew. The Glory remained with us as we rode home.

We rode in to the city, and I saw Pool. She--she looked different. But I couldn't say why. Was I seeing a new beauty because of the Light? I sat silently and watched as Fortress dismounted. She walked up to him, and slowly placed one arm over one of his shoulders, and then the other arm over the other of his shoulders, and looked at him and said, "There is life inside me."

His eyes opened very wide, and then he closed them very tightly, and then he gave Pool the longest kiss I have ever seen.

"Wait," Father Mirror said. "First discharge your duty to our bishop. You will have this life and the next to gaze on the Glory. My guest room is free to you for as long as you need."

I looked at him wistfully.

"The highest oath a monk takes is obedience. That oath is the crystallization of manhood, and when you kneel before me as your father, your spirit will fall in absolute prostration before the Father of Lights for whom every fatherhood in Heaven and on earth is named. And if you are to be in obedience to me, you can begin by waiting to take that oath."

I waited.

The days passed swiftly. Quills and scrolls were given to me, and I inscribed three books. I wrote The Way of Death, in which I wrote about the error as a path, an encompassing way of living death, in which error, evil, and sin were woven together. I contemplated, prayed, and spoke with Fortress and others. Then I wrote The Way of Healing, in which I answered the question, "If that is the path we should avoid, what path should we walk instead?" Then I wrote The Way of Life, in which I left the way of death behind altogether, and sought to draw my reader before the throne of the Glory himself. I wrote:

But what can I say? The Light is projected down through every creature, everything we know, yes, even the Destroyers themselves. But if we try to project upwards and grasp the Light, or even the hope that awaits us, it must, it must, it must fail. "In my Father's house there are many rooms." These rooms are nothing other than us ourselves--the habitations and places into which we invite friend and stranger when we show our loves, and the clay that is being shaped into our glory, the vessels we will abide in forever. The Tree from which we were once banished, has borne Fruit without peer, and we will eat its twelve fruits in the twelve seasons. Yet a tree is smaller than a man, and a man is smaller than--

The temple where we worship, where Heaven and earth meet, is now but the shadow cast when the Light shines through the Temple that awaits us. The Light is everywhere, but we capture him nowhere. He is everything and nothing; if we say even that he Exists, our words and ideas crumble to dust, and if we say that he does not Exist, our words and ideas crumble beyond dust. If we look at the Symbols he shines through, everything crumbles, and if we say that everything crumbles, those words themselves crumble.

I end this book here. Leave these words behind, and gaze on the Glory.

I dropped my pen and sat transfigured in awe. I was interrupted by shaking. "It's time for the Vigil?"

I began to collect myself. "Vigil?"

"The Vigil of when Heaven and earth met, and the Word became flesh."

I opened my eyes. I realized the end of a fast had arrived.

"The books are finished."

"Finished?"

"Finished."

I do not remember the Vigil; I saw through it, and was

mindful only of the Glory. The head monk learned I had finished, and the bishop was called.

Then came the feast. Pool held a son at her breast, and looked disheveled, tired, radiant. Fortress beamed. His Grace Fire spoke on the three gifts given the Glorious Man: Gold, Frankincense, and Myrrh. Gold was a reverent recognition of his kingship, Myrrh a reverent recognition of his suffering, and Frankincense a reverent recognition of his divinity. He turned these three over and over again, blending them, now one showing, and now another. His words burned when he said that in the person of the Glorious Man, these gifts were given to the entire community of Glorious Men.

The feast was merry, and when it wound down, Father Mirror welcomed me into the community. It was a solemn ceremony, and deeply joyful. I swore poverty, chastity, and obedience. I found what I had been seeking when I fled my island. Then I was clothed--I was given the shroud, the cocoon of metamorphosis by which I was to be transfigured during the rest of my life.

After I retired to my room, I heard a knock at my door, followed by quick footsteps. I looked around, but saw no one.

Then I looked down, and saw a gift box. It was empty. Or was it?

Inside was a single grain of Frankincense.

www.ingramcontent.com/pod-product-compliance
Lightning Source LLC
Chambersburg PA
CBHW030815310726
48980CB00006B/505/J

* 9 7 8 0 6 1 5 1 9 3 6 1 8 *